BOOK SEVEN OF THE CITIES WORLD SERIES

THE DARK DAWN

L. D. VALENCIA

Copyright © 2023 L. D. Valencia

All Rights Reserved. No part of this publication may be reproduced in any form or by any means, including scanning, photocopying, or otherwise without prior written permission of the copyright holder.

First Printing, 2023

Printed in the United States of America

Special Thank You to my Kickstarter Backers.

These people helped make this book a reality.

Brian

Gabriel

Angie

CONTENTS

PROLOGUE	1
FILE #1: THE SHADOW ASSASSIN	5
FILE #2: TRIAL PERIOD	12
FILE #3: AN UNPRECEDENTED ATTACK	20
FILE #4: COMBAT MEASURES	28
FILE #5: A LEAD	34
FILE #6: GOOD COP, BAD COP	41
FILE #7: A NEW MISSION	47
FILE #8: THE ESPADA	56
FILE #9: THE ZIGGURAT	62
FILE #10: PHASE TWO	68
FILE #11: VENEZUELA	74
FILE #12: AT DAWN, WE MONITOR	80
FILE #13: THE PARTY	88
FILE #14: DECODING THE DRIVE	95
FILE #15: HER REAL MISSION	101
FILE #16: THE RAVEN	107
FILE #17: ACCORDING TO PLAN	113
FILE #18: TWO AGENTS	120
FILE #19: MISSION FAILURE	126
FILE #20: THE OTHER MISSION	132
FILE #21: EIN	138
FILE #22: CHANGE OF PLANS	144
FILE #23: THE LURE	150
FILE #24: THE CABIN	157
FILE #25: ASSAULT	164
FILE #26: THE SHADOW STRIKES	170
FILE #27: THE FLAME	176
FILE #28: THE NEXT PHASE	181
CHARACTERS	189
ABOUT THE AUTHOR	192

Prologue

Jake rushed out the door and down the alley. He turned around the corner and saw him. His target was running full speed down the street. Jake didn't hesitate, breaking into a full sprint.

The target was moving down the street, bobbing through the pedestrians. He was quick, but Jake was gaining on him. But just then, the target rounded a corner, and Jake lost sight of him. Immediately, he hit the wall at the corner and saw the target had disappeared. Jake punched the wall in frustration.

"Lost me," said a voice in Jake's earpiece.

"Not just yet," said Jake.

Without any hesitation, Jake, who now went by the codename Brimstone, bolted down the street. Although he didn't know for sure, he hoped he was moving in the right direction. If he didn't catch his target, he could never show his face at the Guild again.

As he came to the next intersection, he looked left and then right. Back and forth, again. *Where did he go?*

A hand pressed against his back. The hand was gentle and inconspicuous, but it frightened Jake nonetheless. He turned to see the source of the hand and saw him standing there.

"Gotcha," said Gabriel.

Jake turned his head and bared his teeth for a moment. Through the snarling, he said, "Nice move."

"Thanks," said Gabriel. "I figured you spotted me when I ducked into that alcove. But I guess I just barely got out of sight."

"Nope. I didn't see you."

"All right, Brimstone. You're on my team now. That means it is you and me against Serena. Or Agent Insight, I guess I should say."

"Fat chance we have. She's beaten us every time we've tried this exercise."

"Funny how that works. She comes up with a training exercise for us, and she's naturally good at it," Gabriel said sarcastically.

"If you boys don't hurry up, you won't have a chance of finding me," Serena said through their earpieces.

"Now where could she be?" asked Gabriel.

"I think you should check in the old bakery," she said through their earpieces again.

"Nice try, Serena," said Jake.

"Should we go there?" asked Gabriel.

"Listen, Sentry," said Jake, using his codename. "You know she's laying a trap for us."

"Maybe we go there and lay our own trap."

The two made their way for the old abandoned bakery a few blocks down the way. When they arrived, the place seemed deserted. However, something told Gabriel that Serena was definitely there.

"It's too obvious to go in the front door, so let's go in the back."

The two of them stealthily made their way around to the back, using various objects as cover. There was a large metal door at the back of the bakery. Immediately, Gabriel checked it. It was locked. With a quick flick of his wrist and a pulse of telekinesis, he was able to unlock the door. Jake pushed into the room with a measured amount of stealth. Gabriel was on his heels, scanning the room. When his eyes picked up nothing, Gabriel pushed out with his telekinetic senses. His telekinetic radar as he called it. Nothing was close, but he got a sense of movement up above.

"I think I am sensing something upstairs. Let's go,' said Gabriel.

"On it," said Jake, already moving in that direction.

Ahead, both of them could see stairs. They moved with a slow but steady pace. With their backs together, they moved back and forth. The first would scan a room, and then they would rotate as needed, working in unison. They had practiced this technique more than once. Every time they ran this exercise, they lost to Serena. This time, they came in with a plan, and they were going to win.

Finally, they came to the door where Gabriel had sensed some motion. He looked at Jake, who stood on the other side of the door. Each of them nodded. Jake slowly uncurled his fingers in a silent countdown. One...

Two...

Three! On three, they both barged into the room.

"What?" asked Jake. There was no one in the room. It was completely empty.

"Where is she?" asked Gabriel. He was absolutely certain he had sensed her in here.

But just as they were wondering where else she could be, Serena tapped them on the shoulders at the same time. Gabriel and Jake stood there, faces blank and eyes narrowed into thin slits. Jake's upper lip was barely holding back a sneer, while Gabriel's mouth was drawn into a thin line.

"How?" yelled Gabriel, turning around sharply with a hand on his forehead.

"I knew you would use that TK radar of yours. So, I tapped into your mind and made you think you were sensing movement up here. The whole time I was in the other room waiting for you," Serena said.

"Ugh, you win again," said Jake.

"I think that makes seventeen in a row," Serena added.

FILE #1

THE SHADOW ASSASSIN

Barrett checked his area once again. He stood on the corner of the wall, looking over the edge to see if anything was moving. His enhanced senses didn't pick up anything, but he wanted to make sure. This new gig was paying for a high rise in the city, as well as all of the luxuries a mob boss could afford. And Barrett liked to indulge in every one of those luxuries. He had recently purchased the before mentioned apartment and the biggest, most expensive car at the dealership. Barrett was going to make sure that he had this job for a long time, and that meant using his gifts to keep Mrs. Uppinghouse safe.

After a quick scan, he didn't sense anything so he went back to doing his normal run through. He walked around the perimeter, checking in with each of the different guard towers on the wall. The entire wall was at least a mile around, so Barrett stayed trim doing his rounds. When he checked in with Janyia, she reported nothing unusual. Barrett walked through the guard post and to the adjacent door. There were four guard houses, one on each corner, and the guard house inside the main entrance.

Barrett went to the front entrance and looked down to see the guards at the entrance. He wasn't supposed to just call down to them, as this could raise alarms, so he pulled out his walkie and radioed them. "Guard house five, this is Red Falcon. Anything to report?" he asked over the radio.

"Copy Red Falcon, there is nothing to report down here," said the first guard. She rolled her eyes at Barrett's overly eager codenames. But he was the one in charge.

"Very good. Over and out," Barrett said.

He made a note to have a word with Raegan about rolling her eyes at him. She probably didn't realize that his enhanced senses were so acute that he could even pick up on her rolling his eyes at him. But he would make sure to surprise her with that tomorrow. *Maybe I should fire her,* he thought. *But that would mean a lot of paperwork. I guess a stern talking will do.*

Barrett went to the far corner to take something of a break. He went inside the corner guard post, and he made himself a cup of coffee. Then Chris, the other guard in the room called out, "Aye, I'm gonna use the loo."

Barrett nodded as he smirked. *What a silly word he thought to himself. Why would they call the restroom the loo?* He wondered.

As he sat, he didn't notice the woman coming up behind him. Well, not actually a woman, but it was swirling shadows in the shape of a woman. The shadows passed through the darkness outside, and they crept in as if alive. They were completely outside the sensory perception of Barrett, which was impressive considering his gift. The shadows moved in and sliced into his back.

Shock was the only word for it. More so that he was being surprised, more so at the pain that he was feeling. *How could someone have gotten the drop on me?* His enhanced senses should have made it impossible. But the shadows were completely soundless, set off no motion detection, and were almost completely imperceptible unless you actually saw them, which he didn't.

"Why? Why? Why?" Barrett called out to no one in particular.

A woman watched from the distance. She controlled the shadows, and she quickly finished Barrett off. The last thing Barrett saw was the woman's unusual black hair with a shock of white streaked through it. She spoke into her earpiece. "All right, the watchdog is down. Move in."

Just like that, her team moved into the area. Many of them quickly and easily scaled the wall. In a flash, the guards patrolling the outside wall were extinguished, leaving just the guard house for the main entrance. The darkhaired woman quickly followed suit and scaled the wall. Once she was over it, she looked down at the guard house. They needed to take out the guards before they checked in and realized something was amiss. She rolled around the side and got a visual on the two guards inside. From her research, she knew that these two guards were Raegan and Beamer and neither had defensive capabilities, as they were both energy-based blasters.

Like the shadows that she controlled, she moved silently down the inside of the wall. She was at the door in a flash and pulled out a small mirror. After checking her own reflection for a moment, she held it up to see the two guards inside. Neither of them was looking in this direction. Standing up, she summoned shadow blades and, in a matter of seconds, they were both cut down, unaware of the dark force that had taken them.

"Astrid—I mean Dahlia," said a voice in her earpiece. "Outside perimeter is secure. Permission to move in?"

She looked around to double check that the guards were down. "Move quietly. Madame Uppinghouse isn't the baddest lady in England for nothing."

Her team moved quietly along the outside of the wall. The massive mansion was at the center of the compound. Astrid looked through her binoculars as they approached. To think that this woman had all these resources and she could build herself a military grade compound was impressive. But it wouldn't save her in the end. Not from Astrid and her team.

Like a knife through butter, her team moved to the mansion. Before she arrived, she heard a whispered voice over her earpiece. "Team's in position, ma'am. Waiting on your orders."

"Move in quietly. The longer we can keep Uppinghouse from noticing us, the better."

"Understood."

The team entered the building, their black body armor shadowing them from sight. Astrid arrived at the mansion a few moments after her team. She scaled the wall and climbed to the roof with ease. When she finally reached the roof, she rolled her wrists. They were feeling old these days. She was past her prime, even though she wasn't old by any means. She moved to the central vent. The information she'd collected told her that her target's room would be right about...there. She summoned a shadow and cut through the roof, peeling back the siding and entering the building like a cat burglar. *If only I was just a cat burglar*, Dahlia thought. *But Madame Uppinghouse isn't so lucky.*

Inside, Astrid could see elaborate sconces and tapestries covering the walls. A fireplace with the faintest flickers of a glow was dying on the far wall. She moved to the lush couches and looked around. The madame's interior designer had given her the entire floor plan of the room, so she knew that her bed would be on the opposite side of the room with the fireplace. She moved like a panther, silent and deadly, and approached the bed.

Without making a sound, she stood over the form under the covers. She would make this quick and painless. Astrid favored effectiveness over brutality or pain. She was a knife after all. An assassin. Well, now she was. Before things had changed for her. A part of her thought back for a moment, but she squashed the memory before it bloomed in her mind.

Looking over the sleeping form in the bed, Astrid summoned a shadow to strike and sliced her with a perfect deathblow, narrowing her eyes at the scene before her. The form hadn't stopped moving. It started rolling. She pulled the cover back to reveal a dummy left where the body of Madame Uppinghouse should have been. She looked around.

A woman's voice made her blood run cold. "Well, Astrid. I was expecting you."

She turned to see a false wall open and the old woman walked into the room with a guard at her side. "You see your informant, Mr. Redding. He's really my informant," Uppinghouse said.

Astrid sneered at the revelation. This was why she'd left the Protectorate. All of the politics, in-fighting, and, of course, the backstabbing. She shook her head, as if to shake the thought from her mind. It made her sick. Of course, Mr. Redding would have to pay for this betrayal. It made sense when she thought about it. He wanted Astrid to come here, lose, and then have her enterprise taken out so he could take over. But there was one problem with his plan. Astrid was not going to be defeated. She was one of the most powerful gifted in the whole world, and she had a gift with almost limitless possibilities.

Madame Uppinghouse was now in the room, her guard standing to her left, just behind her. She looked at Astrid like a grandmother looking at a child who had been caught stealing cookies from the cookie jar. "What made you think you could come here and finish me off?"

"Well, you know what I do. Your operation is being taken over by your competitors."

Madame Uppinghouse laughed. "That's rich," she said in her thick British accent. "There's no way I'm giving up my throne that easily."

"Well, that's just fine. I wanted to make this quick and painless, but we can do this your way if you want."

Uppinghouse's guard was able to control the one thing that countered Astrid's gift. Light. But he wasn't able to keep his guard about him, being as young and arrogant as he was and that came back to bite him in the end. Multiple strikes from the front left him in a rhythm. He hadn't taken into account that Astrid could control shadows from a distance. So, when he wasn't expecting it, she shot a shadow spike that caught him in the back. He screamed in pain.

Wide-eyed, Madame Uppinghouse watched as her ace in the hole drop to the ground. Easy victory was slipping from her grasp. Her gaze flitted back and forth from the dying gifted to

Astrid. She couldn't believe it. He should have been able to handle Astrid easily. He'd been so highly recommended.

Astrid wiped her brow in an exaggerated manner. She stared Uppinghouse down. "Well, Madame," she said. "It looks like our business here is just about finished. Any final words?"

Unlike some, she didn't beg or plead. She stood there with a serious, stony expression, awaiting her fate. With barely a muffled groan, she fell to the floor, blood from the wound in her chest pooling around her.

A few minutes later, the rest of Astrid's team entered the room. Astrid, having singlehandedly accomplished the mission, was walking out the door. Reese, her informant, looked at the rest of the team with a smile. "What'd you expect, mate?" he asked. "She's the best."

Morgan, her second in command, fell in step beside her. "How'd it go?"

Astrid turned to face Morgan. Her eyes were green today. *Interesting*, Astrid thought. "She pulled a fast one on me. But I was able to finish the mission in the end."

Morgan contemplated this for several seconds. As usual, Astrid was always to the point. She never said more than she needed to.

"Ma'am, can I ask a question?"

"Morgan, you've been with me for years now. You don't need to call me 'ma'am' anymore."

"Thank you, ma'am," Morgan replied. "Why would we take out Madame Uppinghouse? She was a repeat client."

"Well, Uppinghouse was growing too powerful in her position. In our line of work, just a little bit of chaos is important. If everyone got too comfortable, things wouldn't be good for business."

And with that, she walked out of the building just as the cleanup team was entering. She pulled her old friend, Masque, aside. "Hey, change of plans. Uppinghouse pulled one over on me, so we'll need to rethink our plans."

"Oh, so we aren't going with Plan A?" he asked.

"No, we'll probably be going with Plan C or D. You decide when you get up there."

"Yes, ma'am," he said and then rushed off to catch up to his team who were waiting inside.

A stealth helicopter was landing as she made her way onto the sprawling front lawn. If her hideout had been in a more populated area, they may have opted for a teleporter, but this would do fine. She grabbed her phone and dialed a number. It barely rang once before the person on the other end answered.

"We finished the mission," Astrid said.

"Will there be any ties to us?"

"Not in the least. Our cleanup teams will be taking care of it."

There was a pause. Astrid rolled her eyes. This happened more times than she liked to count. Usually, it happened when the buyer didn't want to fork over the payment. However, this was a slightly different situation.

Astrid finally said, "And my payment..."

"And your payment. We...uh...found her."

"Well, why aren't you telling me, then?" she barked.

"Yes, ma'am. Sorry, but so...Well, the thing is...You aren't going to like where she is."

Her eyes widened.

FILE #2

TRIAL PERIOD

"Insight, do you copy?"

"Of course I copy," Serena said, responding to her codename. *"We're using my telepathic link!"*

Jake peeked through a window, looking down onto the street below. *Not Serena, Insight*, he thought. *"Right, I just mean, are you there?"*

"Yes, I'm still here."

"Where is he?" Jake asked.

"I'm not sure, Brimstone. He hasn't checked in yet."

"I'm getting a bad feeling about this."

"Don't worry," Serena said. *"Sentry is fine."* But inwardly, she wasn't sure. If carefree Jake was on edge, then there was definitely something to be worried about.

Jake shook his head. He didn't like this kind of mission. He was a doer, not a thinker or a planner. And he was most certainly not a waiter. He was about as impatient as they came. His codename, Brimstone, spoke to that. He was a fiery combatant. He rained down destruction on his enemies.

Just then, a third voice came into their minds. *"I'm getting a reading."*

"What is it, Codex?" Jake asked their fourth teammate.

"It's his beacon. He's entered our airspace. But..."

"But what?" asked Serena.

"He's coming in a lot faster than I would have expected. It's like he's still free falling."

"He should be deploying his parachute soon, right?" asked Serena.

"I would have imagined he would have done so already. He won't survive a fall from this altitude."

"Well, obviously. But he isn't an idiot. He knows that."

"Uh oh," said Simon. He was still staring at his screen. Simon Cruz, codenamed Codex, looked at the area and enlarged it. His gift allowed him to control technology just by thinking. As he enlarged the image, he feared what he saw. *"Team, we have bogies in bound."*

Serena's eyes widened. She didn't like the sound of that. Enemies followed Gabriel as he descended. They would soon be turning this mission into a fight. Jake meanwhile was already cracking his knuckles, excited for the chance to let off some steam. He had been sitting around for over an hour with nothing to do. Just waiting for Gabriel.

Just then, they heard the voice they were waiting for. *"Hey guys!"* said Gabriel. *"We got a problem."*

"We know. You have some enemies on your tail."

"I do? Oh man! I didn't realize."

"Wait, if that isn't the problem you were talking about, then what is?"

"I couldn't grab a parachute when I jumped off of the plane. So..."

"Agent Sentry, what in the name of Venus were you thinking?"

"I got the computer drive, and I got out of there. I was under heavy fire, so I had to make a break for it."

"So, you jumped out of a plane without a parachute?" she asked.

"It seemed like a good idea at the time," Gabriel said.

Serena shook her head. She cared about Gabriel a lot. They had been together for a few years now, and they really did care about each other. But he wasn't the quickest when it came to thinking and planning. *What are these boys going to do without me*? She thought to herself.

"All right, new plan. Brimstone, you get in range to provide some cover fire for Sentry. Codex, you help Sentry figure out where he's going to land, and use whatever technology you need to to make sure the landing zone is clear. I mean cars, people, whatever. Make sure they're out of the area. Who knows how hard this impact will be?"

The two instantly got to work completing their orders. Then Serena focused her conversation on Gabriel.

"Sweetie, can you hear me?" she asked Gabriel.

His ears pricked up at that. She'd never called him *"sweetie"* on a mission before. He was either in a lot of trouble or she was just really worried. He wasn't sure which was worse, honestly. "Yes, I'm still here."

"Are you doing all right?" she asked.

"Yeah, I'm fine," he said. Then he thought to himself, *Good, she isn't mad.*

"Good, because if you don't die on this mission, I'm going to kill you."

"Oh, she is mad," he said to himself.

"Now, make sure you focus on your shielding, all right? You're coming in very fast and hard. We need to slow you down."

Just then, Simon reentered the conversation. His voice entered into their minds saying, "All right, good news or bad news?"

"Bad news," Gabriel said.

"Bad news is that if you don't hit a river, you'll likely cause a massive crater in the ground and destroy most of the harbor."

"What's the good news?" asked Gabriel.

"There's a river nearby that you can hit."

"Ah, right," Gabriel said.

"How do I get to it?" he asked. From his perspective, the ground was approaching very rapidly. Gabriel could see a thin, dark line. He was pretty sure that was the river. Or it could've been a road. It was nighttime, and everything kind of blended together in the darkness.

"Use your arms and legs to shift yourself to move to that long, winding pattern. That's the Delaware River."

Simon watched his teammate from the video feed he was tapped into. Gabriel was steering himself away from the river. "No, not like that. The other way."

"How are you seeing me?" Gabriel asked.

"I tapped into a satellite feed so I can monitor you perfectly. Just do what I say."

So, Sentry realigned and moved the other way. His body started to shift in the other direction. He was now on track to land in the river.

"Hey, guys. At this speed and distance, won't that water feel like concrete if I hit it?"

"Pretty much," said Simon.

"Good to know."

"That's why you need to shield up. Or better yet, push against the river. If you can slow yourself, you can lessen the impact. Try and push back the water to slow yourself."

So, Gabriel did what he could. Every few seconds he would focus and push against the water. The force was so dense and powerful that he would move upward, slowing his descent.

"I think it's working."

"Bad news. Those bogies are still on your tail," said Jake.

"Can you take them out?" asked Serena.

"I need a few moments to get them in range. Oh wait, they're deploying parachutes now. This will be like shooting fish in a barrel."

Jake got into position near the lake. He was the closest to where Gabriel was going to fall. Simon could see him on the satellite feed, but he was still worried. If Gabriel didn't get this right, he would not only kill himself, but he could possibly take out Jake too.

Gabriel was getting closer to the river now. He still had to slow himself down a little more and then shield up before he hit the water. He pushed again and hoped that would be enough. Then he saw Jake on the edge of the harbor. Fireballs flew past Gabriel in the air. He hoped Jake's aim was good tonight. Otherwise, they would have a whole new problem after he hit the water. But now, he needed to focus on the problem at hand. With one last push, he slowed himself down and then instantly summoned as much telekinetic energy as he could around himself.

He hit the water like a meteor. The splash sent a large wave powerful enough to reach Jake at the edge of the harbor. As the water hit Jake, it hissed and evaporated. Good thing, he had taken out the enemies on their way down.

Now, they waited. A few seconds passed. Still nothing. Gabriel wasn't coming up.

Brimstone didn't hesitate. He jumped into the water and swam as fast as he could to where Gabriel had crashed. He dove down deep and looked for him. For a tense moment there was nothing. But after a moment that felt like an eternity, he spotted Gabriel. Gabriel was unconscious and surrounded by a small circle of telekinetic energy. It reminded Jake of the tele-stasis field that Serena's mother had been in.

Just then, Gabriel came to and looked around. The field evaporated and water soaked him instantly. Jake grabbed him and helped direct him to the surface since he was so disoriented that he didn't know which way was up. The two breached the water and felt the rush of air in their lungs.

"Do you have the drive?" Jake asked breathlessly.

Gabriel smiled as his heartbeat slowed. "Yeah, it's in my pocket. Let's get back to base so Codex can decrypt it."

***

Back at the Guild, the team was waiting on Simon to decrypt the drive when they were summoned upstairs. Well, everyone but Codex. Gabriel, Jake, and Serena were brought to the corner office on the top floor. It belonged to one of the most important men in the Guild. Someone they only ever saw once in a blue moon, Ein. He was one of the five leaders of the Guild and its founder.

Ivy, the chief intelligence officer, brought them to the small waiting room outside his office. She gave Serena a knowing look and a confident nod as she walked away.

Gabriel looked over at Serena. "What was that?" he asked.

"Oh, I've been working with Ivy for some time now, and she told me this meeting was coming."

"What do you mean?" asked Jake.

"You'll see," said Serena.

After a few more minutes of waiting, Ein opened his office door and looked around. Gabriel and the others sat there as he looked right past them. Finally, his eyes landed on them. "Are you my three o'clock?" he asked.

"I believe so, sir," said Serena, standing to shake his hand.

"Very well, then," he said. "Come on in."

The other two stood and followed him inside the office. It was a simple, white room with very little ornamentation. Most of the other offices that Gabriel had seen had some character or some decor around. But Ein's was so plain that it was almost completely void of any personality. Gabriel stood, while Jake and Serena took the two seats in front of the desk. Ein wheeled around to sit at the desk and then grabbed a large file from the cabinet behind him.

"All right, let's see here," he said, looking over the paperwork. "Well, you three all graduated together from SIA?"

"Yes, sir," said Serena. "We all met during our freshmen year. I'm sure you remember the Drake incident."

"Ah yes," he said. "That was you three, then?"

"Yes," said Serena.

Ein leaned back in his chair. "We are glad to finally have some agents join our team. It's been a while since we got any new agents. But after the Jericho situation a year or so ago, we have definitely improved our image in the Protectorate."

Jake nodded. "Glad to be of service."

"Sometimes I miss being an agent," Ein said with a far-off stare. "You know when I started this job, I was a bigshot. My gift was pretty unique."

Gabriel's ears perked up. He turned from the window and asked, "What's your gift?" Then he followed it up with, "Sir."

"Well, it sounds much flashier than it really is," said Ein. "But I can travel back in time."

"You can travel back in time?" Gabriel asked, his jaw dropping.

Jake sat bolt upright and looked at Ein in amazement.

Ein held up his hands nervously as if he was doing jazz hands. "Like I said, it sounds cooler than it is. Believe me, time travel is not all that it's cracked up to be."

He leaned forward and folded his fingers together. Then he looked down, as if studying the wood grain of his desk. There was an awkward pause for several seconds, while the three young agents looked at each other. Finally, Ein looked back up, obviously trying to hold back tears. He grabbed the pocket square from his jacket pocket and dabbed at his eyes.

"It's cruel, this gift of mine. You can't change the past, you know?" he said. "No matter what you do. That's why I give you this warning. Live your best life today. Never look back to the past and wonder what could have been. Always move forward. Because like I said, you can't change the past. Not even me."

Serena looked up at him and nodded. "Thank you, sir," she said. "That's good advice. We'll remember that."

Ein nodded. "Well, now down to business. It looks like you three have all completed your probationary period. You are now full-fledged agents."

"Awesome," said Jake. "So, we can take on our own cases and stuff?"

"Yes," Ein said. "You will be able to take on individual assignments, go on missions without your overseers, and will have all the authority of a Protectorate Agent. So, use it wisely."

"That's fantastic," said Serena. "So, what's next for us?"

"Well, you will need to go to the Protectorate office in Ithaca, New York," said Ein. "There you will be processed and given one more official evaluation."

"Another test?" asked Jake. "C'mon."

"It's just a psychological screener. They'll ask you some questions and make sure you're handling the stress and everything now. Our agency psychologist will be joining you."

"When do we leave?" asked Serena.

"Report here at seven in the morning tomorrow, and we will have Nyx send you over there."

FILE #3

AN UNPRECEDENTED ATTACK

Axel walked into the alleyway, the rain slicking off his long, black raincoat. He climbed a metal staircase and rounded the stairs three times before he came to the door. Like the instructions said, it was marked with a red X. He tapped on the door and almost immediately it opened. A beautiful darkhaired woman stood there with a terrifying scowl on her face.

"Name's Axel. I was told to meet here," he said.

"Morgan," said the woman. "Come on in. We are about to get started."

Axel followed her into the room. It was a large loft space with an assortment of gear and tech all over the place. He could see someone's high-end computer workstation in one corner, as well as a makeshift sparring ring at the opposite end. A small team was gathered at the far end of the room. That was where Morgan was headed.

Spearheading the group was Astrid. She was holding a small tablet and was clicking something. As Morgan approached, she nodded. Astrid returned her nod and said, "All right, let's begin."

A screen behind her lit up, showing a picture of the Protectorate headquarters. She explained this was the main base for the Protectorate, and they would be sneaking inside to steal something. Axel would have normally been spooked by such an impossible mission. But, this job came from a contact that only sent him certain things. So, the least Axel could do was hear them out. Then he would make his decision.

"Our team will be breaking into the headquarters. We have two guards that Reese has managed to help get us inside. The rest of us will be using these," Astrid said, holding up an ID card.

"How did you get Protectorate ID cards?" Axel asked.

"They're actually fakes," said Morgan. "Reese was able to find someone who can fabricate anything. But it cost an arm and a leg."

Reese nodded. "Literally."

Morgan rolled her eyes and shook her head.

The leader, who Axel learned was called Astrid, continued to explain the mission. They would be stealing a drive with information about the Protectorate agents in the field that they were going to then sell to the Montenegro crime family in Venezuela.

"Whoa, wait," said Axel. "Venezuela."

"Yeah, why?" asked Morgan.

"It's just that place is a little volatile."

Astrid interjected. "It's the perfect place. Because the dictator of Venezuela doesn't allow agencies, there won't be anyone following us there."

That actually made sense to Axel. So, they then went on to his next concern: the escape. However, once again, the leader had it all worked out. "We have Yui for that."

A quiet Japanese girl nodded. She was so still and quiet that Axel had forgotten that she was there at all. She stepped forward. "I will be off site, but I will teleport you all out once you're ready."

"Wait, you're going to be off site?" Axel asked. "Why aren't you going to be there with us?"

"I can't teleport myself, only other people and things. So, if I was there with you, I would be left behind."

"*Ohhhh.*"

Yui just looked at him for a few seconds while Astrid continued her discussion. After she went over the remainder of the plan, she asked if there were any questions. Seeing as how Axel was the only one new to the group, no one else had any. Fortunately, they had already answered his questions so they were all set.

"Well, I guess that's it, team. I will see you all tomorrow morning," said Morgan.

As everyone left, Astrid stayed behind. The base acted as her makeshift apartment. Although most of what she said was true, there were parts of the plan that the others weren't allowed to know. She needed some time to process the heavier aspects of the plan. Alone.

***

That morning, the three youths all arrived at headquarters at seven in the morning. Jake, still wearing his sunglasses, was cursing the insanely early hour. Gabriel and Serena weren't surprised by Jake's early morning complaining. They quickly made their way to the transportation room. To no one's surprise, teams were already meeting in the large room. Many of the command stations were alive with activity.

Gabriel nodded to a team as he passed, sliently wishing them good luck. He didn't know what their current assignment was, but he knew they would probably need it. At one of the far walls, there was a teleportation bay. These sectioned-off areas were for teams to safely teleport back. Each one was clearly marked with a different color, and each teleporter was given a specific color to eliminate any confusion. They were told to report to the blue teleportation bay.

As they approached, a woman seemed to walk out of the blue-lined wall. She was dressed in a tailored black suit with a matching bowtie. Her hair was short and slicked back.

"You three the agents I'm bringing to the Protectorate?" she asked.

"Yes, ma'am," Gabriel said.

"Do I look like my mother?" she said in her sarcastic New York accent. Gabriel's gaze fell, and she immediately felt bad. "Sorry about that." She shook her head and told them to hold on.

They all linked arms, and she walked them through the wall. As they did so, they held their breath. It wasn't required, but it helped in the teleportation process. Some people had a hard time with the change in pressure.

In the blink of an eye, they were in a similar teleportation room. While the Guild's teleportation room had been somewhat active, this one was roaring with activity. People were coming and going constantly. There were also more command stations here, and guards were posted at each one. Before they could even take five steps, three guards were on them.

"Please put your arms out for a routine search," said the female guard.

The new agents all obliged, and they were searched thoroughly. None of the trio thought anything of it, as this was standard operating procedure. Once the guards were done, they were allowed to proceed to the exits. There, they were checked again by a scanner and had their identifications checked. After that, they were finally able to enter the actual Protectorate headquarters.

They came to a large circular portion which appeared to be the main entrance. There was a digital directory showing the different offices and departments.

"This place is like an airport," said Jake. "I've never seen so many people running around like this."

Serena nodded as she scanned the directory for the floor they needed. Gabriel was beside her, doing the same.

"Do you see 'New Agent Processing?'" asked Gabriel.

"Oh, there it is," said Serena. "Floor nine, office thirty-one. Let's move before it gets filled up, and we have to wait for hours."

Serena and Gabriel made their way up to the ninth floor to begin their processing. Jake meandered behind them, looking around like a kid in a candy shop. When they got to the right floor, they found the waiting room labeled "New Agent Processing." They entered to find it more-or-less empty. A few clerks behind desks helped them get scheduled. After a few minutes of waiting, a woman came in to collect Jake. Then a man came in to process Gabriel.

"Galterio Green?" he called.

"That's me," Gabriel said, standing up with his hand up. "But you can call me Gabriel. I go by my middle name."

"You can call me Agent Rail," said the man.

The two walked down the hall to his office. "So, what's your gift, kid?" he asked as they went down the hall.

"I'm a telekinetic."

"Ah, nice. Not bad. I'm an electrokinetic myself," said Agent Rail, strutting a little bit.

"Oh, very cool," said Gabriel.

"Oh yeah," said the agent. "I've been on loads of combat missions. Got promoted when I was only twenty-five. I was on the fast track to becoming a dragoon. But you know how those things go."

Gabriel nodded, but he in fact had no idea how those things went. As they entered Rail's office, Gabriel listened as Rail went on and on about his career. He spared no detail. After almost an hour, Rail was still going. Gabriel finally raised his hand, causing Rail to pause in the middle of a story.

"Agent Rail, what paperwork do you need from me?"

"Oh, right," he said. "Let's see. I need forms I-76 and T-21. Did you sign those?"

"Yes, here they are for you," he said.

"All right. Let me see..."

Meanwhile, a small group of people were meeting behind the headquarters. A darkhaired woman organized her team when they pulled up in the back of a large van.

"All right, everyone. Our IDs have been fabricated by one of Reese's contacts. So, we can get into the building without raising any alarm. However, we still need to be on high alert."

"Why?" asked one of her teammates, some hired help that came highly recommended.

"Once we get to the sub-section, they will have more security and we can't fake those ID's," Astrid said as she wrapped her gray-streaked hair into a tight bun.

"So, we will probably be caught once we get down there?" asked Morgan.

"Not if we stick to the plan," said Reese.

"Let's move, team," said Astrid.

Dressed as security guards, they came to the security entrance. The guard gave them a look as they approached. He didn't recognize these new guards, but they did have the special-issued black two-button suit with the Protectorate emblem on it. He eyed them from behind the secure glass as they scanned their badges. Reese mouthed a silent prayer as the badges were processed and hoped that his contact was able to crack the hyper secure system.

The scanner flashed a red light on and off for seconds, but it felt like hours. Reese was relieved when the green light came on. It meant they would be able to enter the headquarters. Astrid entered first, followed soon after by her two trusted allies, Reese and Morgan. They entered a long hallway. Immediately to their right was a locker room. Reese went into the main locker room first, and there he placed a bag. Then he met his teammates in the hallway. Together they walked around the corner and down to the sub-section.

Normally, no one but a select few highly trusted senior guards were allowed to even come close to this area. However,

Astrid had a secret weapon. Two of the guards were on her side. As they approached, two of the four guards stepped forward.

"I'm sorry," said the first guard. "You aren't allowed to come over here."

Before they could take another step, Astrid nodded at the other two guards. They jumped up and tased the two other guards, who dropped to the ground. Astrid shot a look at Reese.

"Is it—"

He cut her off. "Already taken care of," he said, pointing to the security cameras hanging limply from the ceiling.

Reese's technology-based gift came in handy more than a few times, Astrid thought. *It's very specific, but it can certainly be useful.* "So, when we get down there, we do this quietly. We don't need anyone to know what we are doing here."

However, inside she knew that wasn't completely true. Although her team would help her accomplish her goal, Astrid had a slightly different objective in mind.

Her team was able to get them into the sub-section. Some tech provided by Reese was able to get them into the sub-basement. Down here they could find all the secrets that the Protectorate wanted to keep hidden. Information, operations, agents, you name it, and it was hidden down there.

They entered in quick succession. Now, with her team of five, they began the next phase of their plan and entered the server room. Reese was able to get them inside by turning off the locking mechanism to the door and then Morgan opened the metal doors. In seconds, Reese was at the first terminal, breaking into their secure network.

"I know it's kind of odd, but I have always wanted to break into this place's system," said Reese.

"You're a weird one," Morgan said.

Reese smirked. "You say that like it's a bad thing, love."

Morgan rolled her eyes and walked to the door. She took up acting as a guard, just in case they were spotted before they were able to get away. Astrid watched Reese work. He was able to get into the system in record time. Having a tech-based gifted was practically required to make it in the underworld these days.

"I'm in," said Reese.

"All right, get the intel and let's get out of here," Astrid said.

Reese pulled out a small device. Before Astrid could make it to the door, he called out, "Done."

"Let's move, team," Astrid said.

The small team made their way to the server room door. Morgan gave them the all clear, and they ducked out into the hallway. Instead of going back the way they came, Astrid led the team out a different exit. They found their way through a tunnel that led them to a different portion of the Protectorate. They came to the doorway, which had guards on the other side of the door.

Quickly, Astrid took to her role. Her shadow powers flared to life as she walked through the door. Before the guards could turn, she felled each one in quick succession. The furthest guard had barely turned around before he dropped like a rock.

The team followed her as she made her way up the stairs, most of them not even stopping to check the guards. Reese took a second to observe the downed men. *His skin crawled a little bit. Never betray Astrid*, he thought to himself.

At the entrance, the team waited at the door. Reese once again moved to deactivate the device so they could get out without tripping the alarm. Astrid had them move in small groups, so they wouldn't draw too much attention. They walked out of the sub-section, the secure device in their possession. Now came the hard part.

FILE #4

COMBAT MEASURES

Astrid thought to herself how insane this was. She had just gotten into the most secure facility like it was nothing, and she was going to ruin it. If she was anyone else, she would call herself crazy. *But it had to be done*, she reminded herself.

Astrid followed behind the rest of her team and sighed, a heaviness weighing on her shoulders. She hated the fact that she had to do what she was about to do. However, in the end, it was for the best. Taking a deep breath, she steeled herself for the next phase of her plan.

The team rounded a corner, staggering their walk so they didn't look like they were in the same group. Reese and Morgan were at the front, and just as they rounded the corner, Astrid struck, pushing out with her shadow and slicing at one of her teammates. The man—she didn't know his name—dropped to the ground with a pained scream. At the same time, she used a shadow blade to attack one of the real guards.

"Mission's blown," she called to her team. "Combat measures."

Reese, not being the combative sort, grabbed the small drive and ducked behind a corner. He played the part of a helpless observer, which Astrid was certain he would do. Morgan, however, sprang to action. The other teammates all kicked into high gear. It was fight or die. The Protectorate would not let them escape this.

As expected, several guards started to move into position. Astrid knew exactly how they would move and her experience told her what to do. As the teams rounded the corner, she attacked. However, she wasn't moving to kill. She didn't need a blood bath on her hands—just enough damage to knock them out of the fight. Which, by all accounts, was harder when she thought about it.

The front guards would be tanks, so she avoided them as she began her assault. She jumped over the tanks, and she flung some of her shadow blades at the blasters. They were completely caught off guard, and she immobilized them with little to no resistance. Two brutes came out, ready to tackle her. Summoning her shadows, she formed a barrier. The brutes slammed into it. She shoved them back and then moved onto the tanks. The two tanks were smaller figures.

But what are their gifts? Could they turn into metal, form force fields, or impenetrable skin maybe? Their size meant they probably didn't have strength-based gifts. *Are they siblings? Maybe that means they have similar gifts.*

"Only one way to find out," she said under her breath.

She jumped forward, slashing out with her shadow blades. To her dismay, she was right. Mental-based gifts. She shook her head. She was always right. Also, they probably were siblings because they had the same gift—basic force fields—but they seemed to be focusing their shields so only the front of their bodies were protected. No wait, that wasn't it.

Astrid kicked herself for not realizing it sooner. As she attacked, she realized that one of the siblings was focusing on shielding the front and the other was shielding the back. They were a difficult target now, but it wasn't anything she couldn't handle. Astrid switched up her technique. Instead of targeting one area, she started taking her shots randomly to keep them off balance, forcing them to defend from all directions.

Finally, she snuck one of her shadow spears into their blindspots, and they both dropped to the ground. It wasn't exactly a deathblow, but she didn't have time to finish them off for good.

She looked over and saw Reese firing off shots from where he stood. He was launching small coins using his magnetic manipulation. Meanwhile, Morgan was moving deftly through the guards, making use of her ability to take each one down.

Astrid noticed a security camera at the end of the hallway. It was locked on her, and she smiled at it. With a mocking salute, she rushed in the other direction to meet up with her team. Morgan and Reese were moving back-to-back toward her.

"I think we are clear," said Morgan.

"Then let's get out of here," said Reese.

"First things first," said Astrid. "My welcome-home present."

With that, she shot out a large tendril of shadow and sliced the pillars at the entrance. People screamed when they saw the shadow attack. Stone pillars cracked and started to crumble, crashing to the ground.

"There, now we can go," said Astrid.

Reese was already on it. "Yui, get us out of here."

The three teammates vanished into thin air. Seconds later, they appeared back in Astrid's hideout. Astrid looked around to make sure they weren't being followed. She was experienced enough to know that there was no such thing as a perfect getaway. Not in the world of the gifted. There were gifts that could teleport and dispel other's gifts so there was no telling what was possible.

After several seconds of silence, they assumed they were in the clear. If no one was here already, they probably wouldn't be coming immediately. And Astrid didn't want to be there when they did. So, they began to kick it into high gear.

"Let's move, team. We are moving to Phase Two."

Meanwhile, Gabriel heard the massive cracking sound. The building shifted and lurched. He jumped up from his seat and looked out the door. His overseer, Agent Rail, was looking around as he hid under the table.

"We need to check this out," said Gabriel.

"No, we shouldn't," said the other agent.

"What do you mean?" asked Gabriel. "There's something going on, so we need to act."

"There are procedures and protocols in place for this."

Gabriel looked over at his paperwork. It was already stamped. Rail had finished it up several minutes ago and had just been forcing Gabriel to sit through story after story. But now something important was actually happening, and Gabriel couldn't just stand around doing nothing, no matter what the senior agent said.

"Looks like the paperwork is finished, so I'll be going. Thanks for your time, Agent Rail."

With that, Gabriel was out the door. Jake was already running down the hallway, and Gabriel was pushing to keep up with him. He ran to keep up with Jake, who was moving like a gazelle. Just then, Serena popped her head out of the door where they started. Lucky for her, she had a normal agent overseeing her process.

"What is going on?" she asked.

"Not sure, but we should help get people out of here," said Gabriel.

Just then, the building lurched again. Gabriel widened his stance, but it didn't help much. The building was obviously in dire distress. But to their surprise, it stopped moving. At least, the building wasn't imminently collapsing. Gabriel remained behind while Serena and Jake helped get the people off the floor and down the stairs. Jake went first, acting as a means of defense in case there was some kind of attack. Once downstairs, they realized what had happened.

"Gabriel, you may want to get down here," Serena said using her telepathy.

As quickly as he could manage, he ran down the several flights of stairs and joined them. There were obvious signs of a battle around. Several agents were lying around the ground and some were wounded. In no time flat, the area was filled with more people evacuating the building. Although the immediate danger was over, it was safer for them to clear the area. Gabriel, Serena, and Jake all moved to aid in that capacity.

They passed the elevators that were flashing, "Out of Order" on the panels. Probably a safety precaution. The stairs were the only way in and out. Except for teleporters. Fortunately, there were several on staff at the Protectorate, so they were able to easily clear out the building. That was when the real authorities showed up.

Someone grabbed Gabriel. Before his eyes even focused on the figure, he heard, "Agent Sentry?"

"Wha...uh...yeah," he stammered.

"Are you always this articulate?" asked the figure.

Gabriel, or as he was known in his official title, Agent Sentry, could see a woman in front of him. She had thick-rimmed, hotrod red glasses and wore a black rain jacket over her suit. She had the air of someone in authority, and the flurry of questions that came out of her mouth were too fast for Gabriel to realistically answer.

"Agent, what happened here?" she finished.

"I don't know. I wasn't on the scene when it happened because I was being officially processed as an agent. I just received my upgrade from interim to professional. I don't even have my license yet."

She narrowed her eyes at him, looking upset, like Gabriel's lack of information was his fault. She turned around to see if anyone else could tell her more. Several other people were moving through the crowd, not exactly helping, but they were asking questions and had started collecting those that could give them some answers.

Serena moved over to a different agent. "How can we help?"

"Agent..." the man asked, waiting for her codename.

"Insight, sir," she said.

"We're trying to figure out what exactly happened, to see if anyone saw anything. Once we get that underway, we'll let you know. Right now, we suggest that you help the wounded or dying. Other than that, I don't know," he said, turning to walk away.

As he was walking away, Serena gave him her trademark glare. She noticed the committee members over to the side. They were the ones that were really in charge and the ones that she needed to speak with to find out what was going on.

All the Protectorate committee members were gathered on the front lawn, separated by a few guards and talking frantically. How could this happen? How could someone actually attack the Protectorate headquarters and not only that, but how could they get away? It didn't make sense.

Dexter Romulus was speaking with two colleagues when he noticed the Serena's red hair as she came up to the guards blocking her way. She was asking the guards if she could talk to the committee members, but they wouldn't allow it. Inwardly, he smiled. Agent Insight, as she was called now, had been a thorn in his side for some time now. Over the last few years, Serena and her friends have been interfering with the plans for Dexter's organization, the Oculus.

Then, the other thorn in his side showed up. Gabriel Green. Agent Sentry. Dexter wished he could just finish him off right now. If he had his way, that was what they would have done. But Bartholomew Zeno was certain that they could use him. New agents were much more malleable to the whims of people like Bartholomew. That made them useful. Dexter didn't have the same flair for manipulation as Bartholomew, but he understood the need for it. He was more of the heavy hammer than the whispering word.

He turned to his colleagues when he heard someone say the words he had been dreading. "The agencies will be here soon."

Dexter rolled his eyes   . Now, his secret was in danger of getting out. He needed to make sure he covered his tracks as quickly as he could.

FILE #5

A LEAD

Dexter turned to see groups of agency members rushing to the scene. He could see members of Zulu Tech moving to administer aid to the wounded. He could see the traditional military overcoats of the Cobalt Corp forming a defensive perimeter and surrounding the agents, their trademark sabers at their sides. Then Dexter saw the leader of the Guild coming up to him. He flashed a badge at the guards that were keeping Insight and Sentry away, but Ein's badge gave them pause. He was quickly allowed to join the ranks of the highest level of the Protectorate hierarchy.

Beside him walked Lionheart himself, King of Germania and head of the Cobalt Corp. He didn't even flash a badge. He simply walked past, knowing his presence alone gave him access to this area.

"Where is the security footage?" asked Lionheart, stopping to stab his sword's scabbard into the ground like it was a cane.

Two visibly shaking committee members came over to him. Even though they outranked him in the Protectorate, he still represented the entire nation of Germania. Quickly, he was brought over to the main delegation of committee members who were discussing that very thing. As they began to collect their resources, a third person joined them. It was none other than the founder and head of Zulu Tech with her personal assistant at her heels.

"I would like a command center set up right here so we can begin our work," she said to her assistant.

"Ah, Madame Genesis, it's been too long," said Lionheart. "How are you?"

"Very well, Lionheart. How is your wife?"

"She's well, thank you," he said, his booming voice seeming to have no volume control.

In a literal instant, Genesis's assistant teleported a large, fully functional command center for them. It was a small pavilion with multiple computer interfaces and a table with a built-in computer for the team to all use together. Genesis smirked, taking great pride in her agency's efficiency at accomplishing these types of missions.

Genesis looked to the committee members around her. "My agency will make sure we find any other injured people as well as heal as many as we can."

Not wanting to be outdone, Lionheart said, "My agency will make sure the perimeter is secure, and then we will send teams out to start patrolling the area."

Romulus was the first of the committee members to respond. "Thank you for your support at this time. We appreciate everything you are doing to help, but I am sure our dragoons can handle the situation."

"Nonsense," said Lionheart. "My teams are already in position. Keep your dragoons here to lick their wounds." Although he said that with a jovial tone, the implication was clear. The dragoons, the Protectorate's elite guard, were the ones who had allowed this to happen in the first place. They obviously weren't up to the task.

Romulus understood the verbal attack quite clearly, however, he was skilled enough at politics to not react or to even let it show. "Indeed," he said. "Maybe it is best to allow them time to reassess the situation."

Before long, Ein, Lionheart, and Genesis had gathered around the computer monitor. Ein asked Simon to quickly pull up the footage of the scene. Anyone else would have been incredibly intimidated being pulled for this job, but such things didn't even seem to register with Simon, who was quick to comply and get the feed going. Despite herself, Genesis pursed her lips, trying not to show her annoyance at allowing another agency member to handle her equipment. Likewise, Romulus crossed his arms and leaned back, annoyed that they were allowing a lowly support agent to help, but time was of the essence. His complaints fell on deaf ears.

"All right, there's the file, and here we go," Codex said. Immediately, the video started playing on the monitor. It showed the battle scene in one of the Protectorate hallways. The small group watched in stunned silence as they witnessed the small team of attackers easily handle the guards. Even when the tactical team of dragoons came in, they, too, were quickly dispatched.

"My word, she handled the twins with almost flawless efficiency," said Lionheart, more impressed than upset.

Despite the dig about the dragoons before, Lionheart couldn't help but be impressed with the twins. Their gifts and abilities were well known in the Protectorate world. Seeing this unknown woman dispatch them all with such cold precision was nothing short of remarkable.

Almost out of the blue, the video ended. They watched it again, this time more slowly, trying to piece together better shots from other cameras, and hoping to get a good shot of the woman's face. Agent Codex was pulling some other footage from the system to add to the growing queue of videos they had to watch.

Meanwhile, Gabriel was pacing around the area. Zulu Tech had a monopoly on taking care of the wounded, and Cobalt Corp was already acting as security. So, at the moment, there wasn't much for him to do except nervously pace back and forth. Serena grabbed his hand, stopping him in his tracks.

"Easy there, big guy," she said. "You're going to make a crater in the lawn from all of this pacing."

"Oh, wow, I didn't even realize."

"You want to know what's going on?" she asked.

"Yes, I'm dying over here not having anything to do."

Serena focused her gift, peeking into the minds of the committee members to see what was happening. At that moment, they were watching a video of the same fight from a different angle. Serena was relayed the details to Gabriel mentally so no one would figure out they were eavesdropping. Then the committee members found a video of the culprits coming out of the security doors.

"They were in the sub-section?" said one of the committee members. "How did they get inside?"

"How did they do anything about this, Melody?" said another member.

"What were they after?" asked the one behind them.

"Were they in the records section?" said a different member.

"Calm down," said Romulus. "Let's keep watching before we start jumping to conclusions. We need to keep our heads about us."

After several more shots, the group had seen the whole thing played out. They saw that they were able to get into the security entrance, and then made their way to the sub-section. However, there was a break in their footage, because there are no cameras in the sub-section. Then they continued when they emerged from another door several minutes later. It helped piece together how the initial attack had happened.

"Well, now we know what they did, but we don't know why," said Genesis.

"For now, this mission is a combat one," said Lionheart. "I request mission authority."

Ein put his hand on the large king's shoulder. "Yes, your team would be the best if this was a full-blown attack mission. However, I know something that you don't."

Everyone turned to Ein, their eyes wide and mouths open. Even Serena noticeably flinched at that, unable to catch herself. She refocused her attention to keep up with the discussion.

"I know who this woman is," said Ein.

Romulus's blood went cold for a second. Despite himself, his hands started shaking, and his heart pounded in his chest. He regained his composure and stifled his apprehension. He was in control of this situation and couldn't let this situation spiral away from him, so he needed to play this right. He didn't want to think about the consequences if he screwed this up. The Oculus didn't handle failure kindly.

"Who is it?" asked Romulus, doing his best to act like he didn't already know. He was perfectly aware who she was.

"Her codename was Astrid back in our Dawnstar days," said Ein. "I was her mission commander, and she was one of the best agents I've ever had. Maybe still the best. She could do it all. She could rogue, tank, blast, or brute with the best of them. She was skilled enough to be a seer even, although her gift didn't lend itself to intelligence-gathering specifically."

"So, she's one of our own?" asked one of the committee members.

"*Was*," said Ein after he cleared his throat. "I thought she died long ago, before I started my own agency. I didn't realize she was still alive."

Romulus said, "So you think you should have this mission?"

"I think my knowledge of this agent would give us the best tactical advantage, so yes, I want this mission," he said.

"We will need to discuss this," said another committee member.

"Genesis, could you supply us with a chamber to meet in?" asked Romulus.

"Indeed," said Genesis. However, this time she didn't have one teleported in. Instead, she created one herself. Although everyone knew she'd created the one they were standing in, it was something else to see her make one in action. In seconds, she had created a small barricaded area with a door at the front.

She walked around to the group and patted the structure. "How's that?" she asked. "I made it soundproof, so you'll have all the privacy you want."

She was met with several thanks and even a small applause. The committee members entered the structure and locked the door. Inside, the twenty Protectorate committee members deliberated.

"I say we let the Guild have it," said one of the Australian delegates.

"But the Cobalt Corp has more manpower ," said another.

"Who says one of those two agencies should have it?" said Romulus. "I say we give it to another agency with the specific qualities we need. Maybe Orion."

"But Ein's knowledge of the subject gives them the obvious advantage in bringing this to a speedy conclusion," said the Australian.

Then one of the European members said, "I also think the Guild has the best chance with that information. I say we give it to them."

"But other agencies have a proven track record with cases like this. Wouldn't it be better to give it to one of those?" Romulus countered.

One of the representatives from Asia spoke up. "I think Ein's team will be the best choice since they have a personal investment in this mission. I say we give it to them."

"Let's vote on it, and see if we can come to a consensus," said the European representative.

To Romulus's annoyance, the committee voted to give the Guild the mission. As they exited, he made several more comments, trying to get them to change their mind. However, no one seemed to listen. He made a note to keep track of those who were against him for the next time they needed a favor. In his line of work, someone always needed a favor. He would be sure to make them regret not voting his way.

After exiting the building, they gave the Guild the good news. Ein was relieved. Lionheart was not, however, he understood their reasoning. He walked over to Ein, his imposing frame overshadowing the old man.

"I don't know if this was the right call, Ein. But I understand it. If you need me, let me know. Remember, this attack wasn't just on a random building. It was on our home base. They attacked all of us when they targeted this building. Make sure you get them back for this."

Ein nodded and shook Lionheart's hand. The massive man could have fit both of Ein's fists in a single palm. With that, Lionheart left to oversee his troops. Genesis then also approached Ein.

"Any words of wisdom, Madame Genesis?" he asked as she walked over.

Although several years his senior, Genesis was about as respected a figure as one could be in the Protectorate. The tone and deference he showed her were obvious. She smiled and leaned against the table. With her palm under her chin, she made an exaggerated show of thinking.

"Can't say that I do," she said. "My agency doesn't generally handle missions like this."

Ein nodded in understanding. "Well, I may need your help if this all crashes and burns."

Just then, one of the committee members approached Ein. "Sir, we have a suspect in custody. Would you like to speak with them?"

Ein nodded. *Good*, he said to himself. *At least we have a lead.*

FILE #6

GOOD COP, BAD COP

"So, I say we go with good cop, bad cop," said Serena.

"Which one am I?" asked Zion.

Serena paused for a moment, thinking it was obvious. Zion's natural scowl made her the perfect candidate for bad cop, but she didn't want to say that to her face. So, instead she asked, "Which do you want to be?"

"I guess I can be bad cop. But I don't know if you are up to being good cop," Zion said.

The two agents had been chosen to interrogate the suspect left behind after the attack. Once they found him, he was immediately identified as one of the attackers. Fortunately, he was only unconscious, so they were easily able to stabilize him. Zion and Serena were on their way up to the holding cell as they discussed their tactics. They were able to use the transportation hub since it was a separate building that was only connected by a single tunnel. There they used one of the holding cells to keep the prisoner.

Gabriel and Ein were following them, along with Codex and Foundry. Together, the team made their way to the holding cells. Once again, Gabriel found himself with nothing to do other than sit around and wait for the chance to help out. It was infuriating. He watched from behind as the two agents watched the footage, familiarizing themselves with the incident.

"Wait, show me that part again," said Serena.

Codex flipped the footage back a few seconds and then replayed it. "Here?" he asked.

"Perfect."

They watched the video several times. Serena was confused. *What made Axel go down?* Something didn't make sense. *Some kind of technical error?*

But before they could analyze it any further, the team arrived. Before they went into the room, Serena looked over to Simon. "Codex, I want you to do some digging for me. We need information on this guy. I need you to tell me whatever you can find. All right?"

"Sure thing. I'll get right on that." Without even moving, he closed his eyes and dove into the internet to find whatever information he could. Gabriel chuckled to himself, wondering how often Simon would just close his eyes and surf the web to watch cat videos or something.

While Simon did that, Zion and Serena opened the door to begin their interrogation. Inside, they found the bald man handcuffed to a metal table. He was still wearing the suit with the symbol of the Protectorate on it. Zion instantly went into bad cop mode, rushing over to him and grabbed at his suit.

"How dare you?" she screamed. "You dare put on this suit. A symbol of protection and peace!"

Zion ripped the emblem off his jacket. As she slipped it into her pocket, Serena put a hand on her shoulder.

"Easy," Serena said. "We need him in one piece."

Inside, she wondered if Zion was actually pretending to be so mad, or if that was just her natural disposition. Knowing her, that was probably just Zion being herself. Now, Serena needed to play her part as the good cop. She sat on the edge of the table next to him and eased Zion to the other side of the room.

"So, Axel," she said, getting his name from Codex. "Do you want to tell us why you attacked the one place on earth that would earn you the wrath of every single Protector in the world?"

Axel didn't answer, so she walked over to the door and poked her head outside. "Can I get water for our friend here?" she said in the most sickly sweet voice she could muster.

Gabriel jumped up, eager for something to do. All the waiting around was killing him.

Serena disappeared behind the door once she received the water. By that point, Serena had received more intel from Codex on their little friend. Apparently, he was a high-end mercenary that hired himself out for various big missions such as this.

"So, Axel, it sounds like you are a pretty big name in the underworld."

He didn't respond. Zion tried her hand at threats, but, apparently, he was immune to that method. After being in his position so many times, he didn't seem too afraid for his own wellbeing.

"Listen, I know what you're doing here," Axel said.

"Oh, really?" asked Insight. "What is it that we are doing here?"

"This whole good cop, bad cop routine. I've seen it before, and believe me it doesn't work."

Serena scowled, hiding her annoyance, but she didn't want to admit defeat just yet. Just because they had been found out didn't mean they were out. They just needed to pivot. They needed to find a way to make up for this and still complete their mission. Serena quickly passed that idea on to Zion, who ran with it and began to list all of the things that Axel was going to be tried for, listing every infraction and crime that was going to be pinned solely on him. After she finished, Serena noticed that he was starting to sweat. They were breaking him.

However, just then it clicked. She realized why Axel went down. Ein had explained that Astrid had a unique ability called shadow manipulation. It wasn't a trick of the light or a technical glitch. Astrid was actually using shadows to attack Axel. Axel meant nothing to her. He was just a fall guy. Someone to take all the blame while she ran away.

Serena turned to the door and screamed, "Codex, I need a tablet monitor in here now!"

Immediately, Codex popped into the room and handed her his tablet. She pulled up the video from before—the one of Astrid attacking Axel right before everything went crazy. She queued it up and then played it for him. He sat there, half turned, barely looking at the video. Serena glared at him intently. However, her death glare had no effect on him.

She leaned down close to him, and as she replayed the video, she said, "Look closely this time."

He rolled his eyes but turned to watch the video. His eyes narrowed as he actually saw what had happened, but that was the only reaction he gave. "Do you see what is going on here?"

He didn't want to answer, but she could see his walls cracking. He was just about broken. She just needed to push a little further. "Astrid attacked you on purpose. She stabbed you in the back, literally. So you would be the one that the Protectorate pinned for this whole thing. So you would be the one that was sacrificed."

She paused, letting that sink in just enough before she continued to lay it on him. "She wanted you to take the fall for this, but we both know that isn't true. You didn't plan this thing, right? You're a mercenary for hire. You are just a thug that sells out to the highest bidder. You're not an 'idea' guy, right?"

He was just about there. She could see the vein on his temple bulging. He was about to crack. Now for the finishing touch. "So, why don't you just tell us what you know," she said. "Tell us what she was doing here and what she wanted, and we will tell the Protectorate you cooperated to lighten your sentence."

"Fine," he practically whispered. "I'll tell you."

"Anything you tell us will help us make sure she pays for this, and you will hopefully get a lesser time in jail."

"It was a drive. There were names of agents she wanted, so she could sell them to someone," Axel said, his voice just barely over a whisper.

"Who?" asked Zion, her impatience evident in her tone.

"If I tell you, I want a deal. You get me off for this crime," said Axel.

Serena shifted her stance, trying to look bigger than she was. "I can't promise anything, b ut the more you tell us, the better your chances."

"It was some Venezuelan crime family. I think they were called the Montenegro family," Axel said after a moment's hesitation.

Zion and Serena shared a look. They knew the implications there. Venezuela wasn't a part of the United Nations, and therefore they weren't a part of the Protectorate. In fact, they were so anti-Protectorate that they'd banned any agency activity within their borders. That was probably why this Astrid woman had fled there. Serena looked over at him.

"Thank you for your compliance. I'll make sure my official report mentions all you gave us."

Before Axel could say anything, Zion called in the guards to take him away. At first, he looked at the two women with betrayal in his eyes. The guards grabbed his arms to lift him up, and Axel started to struggle. However, the large guards didn't let that dissuade them. Axel was removed as he looked at Insight square in the face.

"You better get my sentence reduced," he said as they dragged him from the room.

Serena didn't like the thought, but she'd gotten what she needed. Although she didn't exactly feel remorse for the man, Axel. After all, he had committed a heinous crime. He should absolutely go to jail for that, but she would at least make sure to report that he was helpful.

Zion was leaving the room as Axel was dragged down the hallway. She waved sardonically as he rounded the corner. Gabriel, Ein, and Codex were standing out in the hallway, looking at her expectantly. Zion nodded to Serena as she came out of the holding room. Serena sighed heavily before she began.

"Well, do you want the good news or the bad news first?" she said.

"Good," said Gabriel.

"Bad," Codex and Ein said in unison.

"Well, the bad news is that Astrid is going to Venezuela. The good news is we know that she stole a drive with agent names on it, and she's planning to sell it to the Montenegro crime family."

"How is that good news?" asked Gabriel.

"Well, because we know where she is going to be," said Insight.

Gabriel put his arms behind his head and leaned back on his heels, thinking. He knew the situation that this put them in. But before he could even start to brainstorm ideas, Zion spoke up with some good news.

"I may have a way in—" she started to say, but Ein silenced her, surprisingly quick for his age.

"Let's discuss this after we leave. There could be eavesdroppers nearby. We want to keep this as tight as possible."

Romulus peeked around the corner, watching the team leave. He would need to report this to the Oculus. Or did he? He wondered. Maybe he didn't. Romulus had always been the Oculus's loyal bloodhound. He had always done whatever was necessary to benefit and protect the organization, even when it hurt the Protectorate. In the end, his loyalty was to Oculus. He would need to proceed with caution if he was going to take care of this. His position in the Oculus and the Protectorate depended on it.

FILE #7

A NEW MISSION

In no time at all, the agents were back at their base. They had received official jurisdiction and confirmation to act against Astrid. Now, they officially had the mission in hand. Nyx had created a shadow portal to bring them through to their home base.

As he was walking through the portal, Ein called for V and Trei to bring a team to the War Room for their battle preparations.

Insomnia, who was waiting for their arrival, stepped in line with Ein as they walked. The room was the main staging room for mission preparations. Codex had spent hours upon hours outfitting the room with the latest technology so they could be better prepared for their missions. It had monitors, computers, and the latest software to streamline the process.

Just as everyone arrived, Agent Crimson walked over to them. He was about their height, but he wore special insoles to give him an extra inch or two. He didn't like being shorter than people. "Jake, can I speak with you?"

Gabriel and Jake fell back from the group. Although he'd called Jake, Gabriel waited with his friend.

"I said Jake," Crimson repeated.

Gabriel nodded and continued on his way.

"Jake—or should I say Brimstone—we have a lead on our suspect. We are going to be moving in. I thought you would want to join us."

"What, really? Absolutely!"

"You'll have to forfeit whatever mission you were doing. Are you sure you're all right with that?"

Jake looked back just in time to see Gabriel and the other disappear around a corner. He turned back to Crimson.

The senior agent was giving him his trademark half-smile. He wanted Jake to be a part of this mission. It was important to the kid. Heck, it was important to the whole Guild, really.

"I'm in," Jake said.

"Well, let's get a move on it," said Crimson. The two turned around and walked off.

As Ein walked, V and Trei came down an opposite hall and joined their group. Ein started giving them a play-by-play of the situation. Before long, V and Trei were summoning different agents to the War Room. Trei pressed a hand to the panel beside the door, and it quickly read his palm print. In a second, the door opened, and they were inside.

"So, I called up Nyx, Piledriver, and Hardlight," said V.

"Makes sense. Nyx is our only teleporter, and Hardlight would provide a tactical advantage in this fight. Piledriver is, well, good at what he does."

Trei then said, "I am summoning DarkSky and Charm."

Ein nodded in agreement. They already had Insight and Zion with them, as well as Foundry, Codex, and Sentry. When Gabriel heard the role call, he had a thought. At first, a part of him told him to keep it to himself, but another part told him this needed to be shared. He was officially an agent now, so he needed to start acting like it.

"Sir, may I make a suggestion?" he asked.

"Speak up," said Ein.

"Why don't we call up Agent Brimstone?" Gabriel said. "His gift would be helpful, wouldn't it?"

V made a face. Gabriel wasn't quite sure what to make of it, but it seemed like V was trying to hold in bad news. After a slight pause, V said, "Well, yes, his gift would be perfect actually. Unfortunately, he's off on another assignment."

Gabriel nodded. That must have been what Crimson wanted. He must have poached him for another assignment. Well, Gabriel couldn't be mad. Agents did have autonomy to choose their missions and pick up new missions as needed. Sometimes they were assigned, but they always had a choice in whether they went or not. Then Gabriel had a thought. Could Jake have been pulled for *that* mission?

Soon after, the rest of team was gathered. Ein then went to the front of the room, and he powered on the screen. He eyed Codex, and immediately a picture of Astrid popped up on the monitor. Gabriel recognized it from the footage they'd been shown. The streak of white through her dark hair reminded him of a lightning bolt.

Ein pointed to the screen. "This is our target. At roughly eight this morning, she attacked the Protectorate headquarters. We believe this to be a premeditated attack in order to steal a drive with the names of agents on it."

A few agents gasped at the last part of that statement. Ein nodded as the severity of the situation finally landed on them. If she stole this information and it got out, countless agents could be compromised.

"However, we have something of a hiccup in our next step. Astrid and her accomplices have gone to Venezuela."

There was an audible groan from someone in the back when she said that. It was DarkSky. He looked a little shocked at his own response. He nodded and apologized immediately.

"Fortunately, Zion has informed me that she has some information that might help us in our pursuit," said Ein. "Zion, can you share that information with the team?"

Zion stood up from her chair and looked out to face the team. "I have a contact in a Colombian agency. The Espada. We were in the Academy together, and I almost joined the Espada."

Gabriel ran through agency names in his head. He'd studied agencies extensively, so he was certain he knew of them. That was it. They were a more combat specific team in Colombia that fought against cartels and other gangs in South America. Since this agency was in a neighboring country, maybe they would know how to get to the Montenegros.

"So, you think this contact will be able to get us into Venezuela?" asked Trei.

"Yes, I believe that the Espada have had issues with the Montenegro family before, and they know where they are. As for sneaking into the country, if anyone does know how, it would be the Espada."

"So, you are suggesting we break international law to get into Venezuela and try to acquire this woman?" asked Trei.

"Technically, we aren't breaking the law by being there. However, the Venezuelan government just doesn't acknowledge our authority. So, we can be there, but we just might be forced to leave if we're found to be operating in the Venezuelan borders," said Codex.

Trei was biting his lip as he felt uneasy about this. Codex's response didn't seem to have the desired effect.

"Anyways. I'm just making the team aware of a potential resource. What the team leaders decide will be what I do," she said and then sat down.

Trei looked somewhat uneasy. He folded his fingers over his face, covering his mouth. Gabriel knew he was thinking, playing around with the thought in his mind. Trei was the perfect soldier. He didn't like the idea of going against the book. The law was against them on this, and that was something that he would have a hard time overcoming.

"All right team," Captain V said, standing up. "The team leaders will convene for a meeting, and Zion will make contact with her associate. Be back here in fifteen minutes."

With that, everyone left except for the three captains, Zion. Gabriel, Serena, and Codex, who all met up in the breakroom downstairs. They each grabbed a cup of coffee and sat around the table. After a moment of silence, Serena finally spoke up.

"Well, this isn't how I expected this day to go."

"No kidding," said Gabriel, sipping at his hot drink.

"Why not?" Simon looked up from his phone.

"What do you mean?" Gabriel asked.

"In this line of work, there aren't many days that go exactly like we plan. You will have to get used to that," he said.

"Yeah, but it sucks that we didn't get to even celebrate our big day. Instead, a psycho killer attacks the Protectorate, and we end up on the assignment," said Serena.

Simon looked at her, unsure. "When you do the math, it isn't that odd. It was a distinct possibility that your day would end with a mission being thrown on you." He took a long sip of his coffee.

Although Simon didn't see his words as anything other than obvious and mathematically sound, Serena was getting heated. She rolled her eyes, and Gabriel could tell she was getting upset. Before he could say anything to calm her down, she said, "Well, not everyone is as married to their job as you, Codex."

His codename came out like it was an insult. A curse. Then she got up and walked out of the room.

Gabriel hung his head. *Can't we all just get along*, he thought, sighing deeply.

"What did I say?" Simon looked at the door where Serena exited.

"I don't think she wanted you to give her a reason or explain it, Simon."

"Why not? She posed a misnomer, so I was correcting her assumption."

Gabriel ran his hand over his face. "Uh, yeah, but I don't think she wanted the situation to be explained. I'm pretty sure Serena knows that there is always a chance she will be called away to a mission. She just wanted you to say 'Yeah, what a bummer' and move on."

"So, she wanted a certain response from me?" Simon still looked confused.

"Kind of."

"Hmm, I don't get it," Simon said.

"I mean, no one does," Gabriel said, signing heavily once again. "It's just a social thing."

Simon was silent for a moment. Then he plainly turned and said, "I don't get people."

"Neither do I, man. Neither do I."

In a flash, the fifteen minutes were over, and the team was reconvening in the War Room. Zion was up at the front with Ein. As everyone was filing in, they could see her standing ready. Gabriel and Serena sat down, knowing full well what they had decided.

"Well, team. Thanks to Zion's contact, we have an in down in South America. We'll be sending an away team to meet with the Espada. If we're lucky, we may have gained access to the Montenegros and in turn, Astrid."

Just then, Foundry raised a hand. "Sir, why were we given this mission? Why not someone in South America or a more specialized team?"

Ein sighed heavily. "Well, that's the next thing I wanted to tell you all. Astrid was a former agent of mine. Back in the day, I was an agent handler for Dawnstar, the first agency. But there was a mission that went sideways. Afterwards, we thought she died. There was no sign of her. We had a funeral, and we moved on. But, somehow, she survived."

He paused. The tension in the room was palpable. No one said a word.

"But I believe she harbors a grudge now. I think she is back for revenge. I believe that whatever she is planning, she wants revenge on the agents who let her down or the Protectorate as a whole."

Again, there was a pause. No one knew what to say. No one, except for V. He stood up and walked over to the front of the room. He stood beside Ein for a moment and then turned to the group and said, "That's why we cannot allow her to succeed. So, let's go over our team."

Ein nodded. "As usual, Captain V has appointed a well-rounded team to send on this mission. We may be operating off the books a little on this one."

Just then, Gabriel realized that Trei was no longer in the room. He must have disagreed with working off the books. His soldier side couldn't get over that fact, it seemed.

"Sentry," V said, immediately shaking Gabriel out of his thoughts. "You and Foundry are our tanks, understand?"

Both of them nodded and said, "Yes sir," in unison.

"DarkSky and Hardlight, you two are going to be our blasters, all right?" Ein said.

"Zion and Piledriver are our brute, being our major physical combatants. Serena and Charm, you two will be our sages, because we will be working on gathering intelligence. Nyx is our rogue. Codex is our seer. He will oversee the operation from afar. Overall, I feel this is a well-rounded team," V added.

Ein gave their final orders. "You will meet with Zion's contact in Colombia in Bogota and work out whatever they need in order to help us take our next steps. Then you'll get into Venezuela and retrieve Astrid. Any questions?"

There were none. Now that they had their orders, they were given permission to leave. They quickly made their way to the locker rooms. Right next to the locker rooms was the armory, where Duo worked on perfecting their fashionable suits into something more like armor. Over the years, he had found a way with his alchemy to blend metal into fabric, making their three-piece suits practically impenetrable.

As they entered, Duo gave them a breakdown of their suits' latest modifications. "For some of you, I've used a slightly denser material for their suit jackets. Others have requested less protection, so yours are lighter."

Zion gave him a nod.

"Also, I've made these white button-up shirts perfect for under your suits," Duo finished.

"How so?" asked Gabriel. "More padding, lighter armor, or what?"

"No, they breathe really nicely, so you won't sweat."

"Ah."

"Best of luck with your mission, team," Duo added as they walked into their locker rooms.

As they donned their finely made suits, Gabriel noticed the battle scars on many of his teammates. So many of them had wounds that showed years of service. It was a mark of honor that many of them wore with pride. DarkSky, who had a long gash down his right side, noticed that Gabriel was looking.

"Got this when we took down the Shuki crime syndicate a few years back," he said. "It's probably pretty gross, but it's great for striking up a conversation with the ladies."

Gabriel smiled and touched the small scar under his eye. He'd received it years ago when he and Jake were fighting. That semester, Jake had been manipulated by a man named Pius, someone affiliated with Dr. Drake and a secret group called the Oculus.

Gabriel shook his head. Now wasn't the time for thinking about the past. He had to quickly assemble his suit. First, he put on the standard white button-up shirt and then he placed the vest over his shirt. Normally, this felt constricting, but somehow, Duo had made the more material durable and flexible. He'd blended the best materials to make something completely perfect.

Next, he put on the specially crafted pants. Not only did they fit perfectly, but they were comfortable too. Gabriel wondered if he could have Duo make all of his clothes for him. He shook his head. Asking his boss to make him clothes probably wouldn't go well, so he decided to just enjoy the perks of the uniform. It was hard to believe that the soft material was actually specially designed to be protective enough to withstand a blast.

Lastly, he put his arms through the jacket and sured it up with a few adjustments. Then he grabbed his tie and quickly finished the knot. He checked to ensure his tie was tied in a New Windsor knot. With a quick nod, he turned around to leave. Now he was ready for whatever this mission entailed.

FILE #8

THE ESPADA

The team reassembled in the hallway and walked down to the transportation hub. Gabriel looked around at his team as they walked. Zion, as always, looked ready to fight. Codex wore his shirt with the tie loose like he usually did. Because he wasn't in the field, he usually would forgo wearing a suit jacket. It was nice to know that he wasn't working alone. He had a team to back him up. Now he was a real agent.

Inside the transportation hub, Nyx summoned her shadow portal and they were off in seconds. Gabriel wasn't sure if they had shown her where they were going, but they ended up inside a similar room on the other side. However, this one had a brighter look to it. Instead of the simple gray color, this one had banners with the agency upon them. The Espada's sword emblem was on each one. They were approached by a tall woman.

"Zion, it's good to see you," said the woman.

Zion put out a hand to shake the woman's, but she quickly wrapped Zion into a warm embrace. However, Zion didn't hug her back, keeping her arms down at her sides. The whole exchange was incredibly awkward. But then again, Zion wasn't one to show affection. Not after her loss.

"Katana, how are you?" Zion asked.

"I've been great. Things are going well in the Espada," she answered.

From a distance, Gabriel saw a slight resemblance between them. It wasn't the kind of resemblance between family members. More like the similarities one gets from having a similar style or personality. The two women spoke for a few minutes, leaving Gabriel to believe they had been in the Academy together and had been on missions together.

"I'll tell Claymore that you are here," said Katana, and then she walked off. A few seconds later, she was back with a large man who had biceps bigger than Gabriel's head. His eyes widened as he saw the mountain of a man approaching.

"Zion, what's new?" the man asked, his gravelly voice reaching them from the other end of the hallway.

Zion walked over and gave him a handshake. She called her team over. They approached and met the contact. Quickly, they were all whisked away to a meeting room where they were introduced to the team they would be working with during the mission.

"This is Dart. She's a speedster," said Claymore. He pointed to a shorter woman with a rounded face. Her head was shaved, and she wore goggles. She looked like an Olympic swimmer.

"And I'm Katana," said the woman they'd met before as she tied her long hair back into a tight bun. "I'm a telekinetic. I specialize in weapons combat."

"I'm Claymore," said the massive hulk of a man. "I'm a metal form."

Then their team leader stood up. "I'm Gladius," he said. "I have enhanced strength and durability, and I will be leading this mission."

Zion nodded. Gabriel didn't quite understand, but based on what he could put together as they spoke, the Guild was doing the Espada a solid by helping them. This meant it was still an Espada-led mission. In return, the Guild was getting their help.

So, would the mission still be a Guild mission? Gosh, Protectorate Agency relations are complicated.

"So, in exchange for helping, you get into Venezuela. We need you to help us take down a local despot," said Gladius. "I've been working on this case for a long time, gathering evidence and witness testimonies. It's been a long time coming, but I finally have enough evidence to bring this guy down."

"What's he been up to?" asked Gabriel.

"Well, essentially this guy runs an energy company for the whole area. The cheapest energy in the whole country, and because of that, he's run a few others out of business. But this is where it gets a little shady."

Gladius paused, building up the suspense. Gabriel couldn't handle waiting any longer, but before he could get too antsy and interrupt, Gladius finally continued. "This tyrant gets kids with energy gifts and uses them to power his generators. However, he pays them almost nothing. The kids are given barely enough to survive, and some are coerced to work for him with threats of violence or having their families hurt. It's almost slave labor."

At this point, Gabriel was practically fuming. Smoke was all but pouring out of his ears. Whoever this man was, he needed to pay.

Zion spoke up. "So, what do you need from us? How can we help?"

Gladius pulled out his paperwork, a thick folder with sticky notes all over it, and plopped it down on the desk. "This is all the evidence we have on him. We're going to be issuing his arrest today, but we're worried."

"What do you mean?" asked Codex.

"We have reason to believe this man won't go quietly. Even with our resources, we haven't had many agents sign up to take on this mission."

"What, why not?" asked Gabriel, leaning forward as if ready to attack on site.

"Well, our suspect, Sergio Valdivia, essentially owns this part of the country. No one goes against him since he practically owns the power in the area. If you challenge him, he'll just turn off your power."

"So, you want us to go with you to stop him?" Zion balled her hands into fists.

"Not exactly, but maybe. We have a warrant for his arrest. If we're lucky, we get him to come quietly, and we move on with our down. If we are unlucky, he resists."

"That's when we come in?" she asked.

"Exactly."

So, it was agreed that the Espada agents would move in first to issue the arrest, however, the Guild agents would be nearby to jump in if Valdivia didn't come quietly.

Outside of the compound, where Nyx teleported them, was a massive jungle scene with a gigantic pyramid practically lifting up out of the canopy. As Gabriel examined it, he realized it was more like a ziggurat with huge tiered sections. Gabriel couldn't help but be impressed. One of the benefits of the clean energy that the gifted could provide meant that city and nature could exist side-by-side.

They were right outside the massive walls of the facility. Large signs in different languages covered the wall, warning to keep off the property. Behind them was a long road in some disrepair. As they arrived on the scene, Gabriel could hear the Espada agents talking. They didn't sound hopeful that the suspect would surrender. In fact, one agent pulled Gabriel aside and told him to have his shields ready, because this was, for sure, going to be a battle. Gabriel and his team got into position immediately.

The other team entered the compound. Gabriel could see them approach the guards, who were stopping them. From his vantage point, Gabriel could see the guards looking sternly. The guards were shaking their heads as the Espada team was speaking. Despite their warrant, the guards were holding fast.

Gabriel felt a growing unease. *Would these guards try and stop them?* He wondered. He noticed that he was chewing on his lip to the point that it was bleeding. He licked the blood and looked back to the conversation. At this point, the guards were escorting them into the premises. Even still, he readied himself to prepare a shield, like he was advised.

Gabriel spoke over their telepathic link. Serena, however, was straining to keep everyone connected. Not only was she connecting their Guild team, but she was connecting the Espada team as well. She had never pushed herself to interlock so many consciousnesses before. It was a little draining to say the least. In fact, she was positioned further away because she could barely stand with the mental weight.

She was listening in on the conversation that Gladius was having with the guard. After a heated debate, they were now speaking cordially. At least for the moment. However, Serena was also becoming somewhat unnerved. The guards's movements were tense as they walked.

Just then, the front entrances opened. Out walked the man himself, Sergio Valdivia. He was a massive man with a round belly that spoke to the fact he never missed a meal. He had thick, curly black hair and a full mustache.

With arms out like he was greeting old friends, he said, "Agents. Protectors. Welcome to the Zigura Energy Company, the cleanest energy in the world!"

He spoke with such gusto and energy that it was hard not to think he actually believed those things. However, Agent Gladius and his team weren't swayed by his words. They stood together, keeping a tight formation, but they didn't move any closer. They all wanted this to go down without a fight. There was no way to guarantee this wouldn't end in a bloodbath.

"Hello, Sergio Valdivia. I am Agent Gladius with the Espada Agency of the Protectorate. We need you to come with us."

"What?" Sergio held his hand to his chest like he was offended. "Whatever for?"

"We have evidence that you've been using underage gifted to power your energy systems. We also have reports that you've been coercing these minors into working for you. Because of these actions, we are going to need to bring you in for further questioning."

"Sir, I can assure you that I haven't been doing these things. You can rest assured that Sergio Valdivia is a man of the people. I live here. I work here. I love it here. These are my people. I would never hurt them or exploit them."

Gladius mentally rolled his eyes. In his experience, whenever someone referred to themselves in the third person, it was usually a bad sign. He needed to keep the subject calm though. The whole situation could spiral into a massacre if they didn't keep this under control.

"Sir, if you are innocent, then you have nothing to worry about. We just want to speak with you about these allegations. Hopefully, we can get this resolved and have you back home by tonight."

"But what about the company? If I'm not here, who will manage the business?"

"I'm sure they'll be able to manage without you for a few hours. If you could just come this way, we can get going."

Gadius took a step to Sergio, but that was as far as he got.

"Attack!"

Then everything spun out of control.

FILE #9

THE ZIGGURAT

Four teams fired down on the agents from the upper balcony of the building. They were all gifted raining down blasts of energy, fire, and all manner of projectiles. One was even firing off large spikes that protruded from their arms.

The Espada took immediate action. Explosions from the ground threw dust and smoke into the air. The area became a war zone in the blink of an eye, but their training kicked into gear. They all scattered in different directions, hoping to disorient the blasters long enough for them to get to cover. Gladius covered Katana while they darted away. Dart was already ducking behind the wall while Claymore moved in the opposite direction. Unlike the others, he was fine taking direct hits.

As the explosions went off around them, the Guild agents were using a shadow portal to engage the enemies. Gabriel threw up a shield to deflect the energy blasts from Sergio's goons as DarkSky summoned a massive bolt of lightning down on them. Foundry went on the offensive and ripped a portion of balcony away, causing several of the shooters to fall to the ground. As she took care of those guards, more started pouring out of the main entrance.

Thinking quickly, she focused on the metal doors and slammed them shut. For a quick moment, she was relieved. She had stymied the guards. However, it was short lived, because a moment later, they broke through the side windows. They jumped into the courtyard, continuing their attack.

She looked over to see Sentry moving into position as well. He was holding out his telekinetic barrier. Although she didn't have to, as somehow she knew he was there. She still wasn't quite used to this mental link of theirs. It was still comforting to know she had some backup on this mission. There were so many enemies pouring from the building. The Espada certainly undersold the severity of this mission.

Gabriel looked over to see the blasters pouring from the building. Before they were even all out, many were firing off energy blasts or projectile beams. It was like Sergio hired any and every blaster in the whole country. And the courtyard was filled with them. The energy blasts were coming from all angles. Gabriel was holding a shield around the team while they got to the Espada members, allowing them to regroup. But now they needed an attack plan.

"Team, what's the plan?" Gabriel called out through the telepathic link.

"We need to back up and regroup," Foundry called.

"No, we should press the attack," said Zion.

"Hello, can you hear me?" Gladius asked. *"This is an Espada mission, so we are going to call the shots for this one."*

"Understood," Tension was evident in Zion's tone. She winced. It was hard to hide one's feelings when they were literally in each other's heads.

"I say we fall back, give them a false sense of confidence, and then we push back.," Gladius said.

"Yessir," said Gabriel. With Foundry and Gabriel's help, the two teams started to fall back. Gabriel held up his telekinetic shields for as long as he could, relieved when they made it around the corner. He dropped the shield once they were safely

behind the wall and felt like he could finally breathe. He took in several shallow breaths in a row. Foundry was at his side.

"You all right?" she asked.

"Yeah, I think I forgot to breathe for a second there," he said. "But I'm fine."

Meanwhile, Serena was struggling. She was so far behind that the rest of the away team couldn't see her. The strain of keeping so many minds intact was starting to hurt, but she needed to focus and keep it together. No matter what, she was going to hold this.

Over their mental link, Gladius told them to hold position for a few minutes. The two teams complied. The barrage of attacks slowed until, finally, it came to a stop. Gladius smirked. "On my mark. Five, four, three..."

When Gladius got to one, DarkSky lifted into the air and rained bolts of lightning down into the center of the courtyard. The ground exploded, creating a crater, as guards flew into the air around them. Gabriel and Foundry were leading the attack as Claymore and Gladius followed.

Then something unexpected happened. The group's attacks, once unified and in sync, were now disorganized and sloppy. Gabriel was the first to pick up on it.

"*Serena!*"

Their telepathic link was gone. He didn't know if she could hear him or not because she didn't answer back. Nothing.

Before he could turn around, putrid, green energy sent him into the dirt. He shot back up, wiping the dirt from his mouth. Gabriel focused his energy and pushed his attacker, sending him flying backward into the crowd of other guards. They all crashed to the ground like dominos.

I don't use my telekinetic powers to attack often, but that guy had that one coming.

As he turned to run, another guard launched a bolt of lightning at Gabriel as if it was a spear, but he was able to deflect it. He mentally sighed in relief and made a note to thank his instructors at the Academy for drilling him on reactionary timing. That one came in clutch right now. However, the guard didn't let up. She summoned another one and threw this one at Gabriel as well, but it defused the telekinetic shield.

"Get out of my way!" he screamed.

He rushed at her, using his TK shield like a wrecking ball. He slammed into her, bulldozing her into the ground behind him. She landed head over heels and then rolled several more times before stopping. Gabriel didn't even look back to see if she would chase him. He was dead set on getting to Serena. At that moment, he didn't care about the mission or the guards in his way.

To his left, he could see Hardlight blasting guards from behind Claymore, who was acting like a human shield. The two were working well in tandem, despite not being mentally linked anymore. To his right, Nyx created a portal for Zion—who was getting bombarded by energy users—to drop through so she could get away. She then made another that allowed Zion to drop down on the guards. Zion felled them with ruthless efficiency, her psychic blades swinging with the beautiful, flawless skill of a ninja. However, her speed was what set her apart. She landed her blows so quickly that the guards were down before they even knew what had happened.

Broken bits of asphalt slid under Gabriel's feet as he ran through the gate and onto the main road. A break in the fence caught his attention. His eyes widened.

Three of the guards and Sergio Valdivia had Serena in a stranglehold. *Agent Charm is supposed to be acting as a guard! How did they...* But then Gabriel saw that Charm was on the ground behind them.

"Well, Mr. Agent Friend," said Sergio. "Don't move a muscle, or your friend here will have her neck broken."

The guard holding Serena put a menacing hard behind her neck as Sergio talked. Gabriel froze in place, holding out his hand.

"And don't think I won't notice, friend. My gift is super acute hearing. I can hear everything from the people hiding inside my building ot the sound of my enemy's muscle movements."

"Is that how you found her?" Gabriel asked.

"Indeed. I could tell we had someone in the back hiding, so I snuck off with my guards to see what it was. I know I cannot beat you outright, so I figured a hostage was my best bet to get out of this situation alive."

"Well, let's make a deal then. You let them go, and you walk out of here. Sound good?"

"Possibly," he said. "But I think I'll take one of them with me to keep just in case you come after me."

Sergio looked at Serena. Gabriel could see the evil in this man. For him, ending Serena's life would be just as easy as breathing. This ended here and now. Gabriel flinched, and Sergio looked over to him.

Sergio waved his index finger back and forth. "No, no, no. Don't you move."

Gabriel focused his mind. He would have to do this without tensing even a single muscle. Without changing his breathing.

Although his gift was all mental, he used his hands as guides and his breathing to regulate it. Doing this completely without moving would be a unique challenge. But he had to try. He knew beyond a shadow of a doubt that if this man got away, he wouldn't let Serena live.

But what to do? That was the question. He needed to figure something out quickly. This situation had a few precious seconds before it was all over. Of all the people he needed to worry about, the guard with his hand at her neck was the biggest, most immediate threat. At least immediately. So, without moving a muscle, Gabriel pushed out with his mind. He wrapped his energy around that man's hand and pulled. The guard's arm snapped back, frozen in the air. After the initial shock wore off, the man pulled back against the telekinetic energy. His strength was immense, almost enough to rip free, but Gabriel doubled his effort. This time, he pushed back against the man's chest. The second attack sent his opponent flying backwards into the other guard. Both dropped to the ground, the second completely hidden underneath the strong man's massive bulk.

The third guard, a female, summoned energy seemingly out of thin air. Gabriel had seen a gift like hers once before. She could pull from the solar energy from the sun.

He had to time this right. Too early, and he would leave himself open. Too late, and he would be rocked by a solar blast that could incinerate him.

She moved her hand, and he jumped forward into a dodge roll. Her blast sailed over his head. The heat was so intense, it actually singed his hair as he moved. He came out of his spin and pushed out a telekinetic wave so strong that the woman went flying into the nearest tree The impact left a large crack in the bark. She dropped to the ground, unconscious.

Sergio's smug expression had disappeared. A minute ago, he'd been smiling, certain he would get away with this. But now, his face was a mix of shock, terror, and confusion. Gabriel smiled on the inside, but on the outside, he was all business.

"Sergio Valdivia. You have the right to remain silent. By the authority granted to me by the Protectorate, I am bringing you in for questioning because of the unlawful actions of you and your company," Gabriel

He pulled out his handcuffs and restrained the man. Fortunately, Sergio's gift wasn't combat specific so he wouldn't be dangerous from this point on.

FILE #10

PHASE TWO

Once Valdivia was restrained, Gabriel turned his attention to Serena. "Agent Insight," he called. "Are you all right?"

Serena was holding her head. "Mostly, just my pride."

"What happened?"

"I don't really know. I was so focused on keeping the link up between everyone on the team, I was almost completely unaware of anything else going on. I was practically blind and deaf."

"So, he snuck up on you two?"

"That's my guess. We can check in with Charm."

Gabriel leaned over her and tapped her cheek. She immediately came to. "Sentry, what happened?"

"That's what I was about to ask you," he said.

"I was looking out toward the battle, keeping an eye out for any guards, but they must have gotten behind us or something," Charm said, getting up with Gabriel's help. She rubbed the back of her head and looked at Serena, realizing by the red marks around her neck that she had been attacked as well. "Insight," she said. "I am so sorry. I really blew that one. Can you ever forgive me?"

Serena nodded. "Yeah, we got lucky this time. Sentry moved quickly." She raised an eyebrow at him. "How did you know?"

"Well, after a while, I realized our mental link was broken. So, I knew something was up. I rushed over here as quickly as I could."

"Well, I appreciate it. Normally, I would have called one of you to help, but I was so mentally taxed that I could barely even think."

"Well, I need to get back to the team." Gabriel darted back to the gates to join the fight only to realize that the team had everything in hand at this point. Most of the guards were restrained or unconscious. Foundry had used metal pieces from the balcony to wrap around some of the guards when they realized they didn't have enough handcuffs.

Just then, one of the guards that had been lying on the ground stood up and darted for the back of the building. Gabriel knocked him down with a well-placed telekinetic pull at his legs. The guard fell to the ground and slid several feet. Piledriver was on him in seconds. With one hand, Piledriver picked him up and held him over his head.

"Not so fast, buddy," he said. "We got a special place for people like you."

Gabriel exhaled a deep sigh of relief. He'd been worried that something may have happened while he was away, but fortunately, the team seemed fine.

Except for Zion. His eyes widened. She was stomping over to him, her face pinched in a stern expression that was hard to miss. She grabbed him by the collar and looked him dead in the eyes.

She spoke in a tone that wasn't a whisper exactly, but it wasn't loud either. "You have five seconds to tell me exactly what happened there, agent. Where in Venus's name were you?"

Gabriel stood at attention. "I was moving to the aid of one of our teammates. Agent Insight was in need, so I rushed to help."

Zion looked over Sentry's shoulder to see Insight and Charm walking in their direction. She could tell that the agents were a little worse for wear. When they arrived, they confirmed that Agent Sentry did in fact help them.

She pursed her lips. "That still doesn't excuse the fact that you left the rest of your team! What if *they* needed you?!"

"Insight is important to my team." Sentry crossed his arms over his chest. "I needed to make sure she was okay. My teammates depend on her gift. It's vital to our missions." He bit his lip. He didn't want Insight thinking that he only saved her because of her gift. That wasn't the reason at all, but Zion seemed to think leaving the rest of the team for one member was unforgivable.

"That may be, but it still doesn't excuse your reckless actions." She turned away from him. "You could have cost us everything. Think about your whole team next time."

By that point, the Espada were gearing up to enter the building. The other team needed to join them, but first came the awkward decision of figuring out who got left behind to watch the captives. At first, Gabriel was certain Zion was going to pick him, if for no other reason than to make a point. However, she passed over him and picked DarkSky and Hardlight since they were the blasters. They would be best suited to take down anyone who tried to escape.

With that, the team entered the building. Claymore and Gladius took the lead, walking as if they expected more guards to attack at any moment. Despite their careful movements, no one attacked. No one else seemed to be present. It was like the entire staff had been made up of Sergio and a bunch of guards.

They scoured the halls for any signs of people. However, most of the offices and work areas were empty. Most looked like they had been empty for some time. It was like they were set up for show and no one actually worked here.

"Anyone else feel like this is some kind of weird ghost hunt?" asked Gabriel.

"Seriously, this is weird," Serena added.

"Where are the workers?" asked Charm.

"I'm starting to suspect that the entire workforce of the power plant is the guards to make sure that the energy-based gifted stay in line," said Gladius.

"If this isn't proof, I don't know what is," said Zion.

"Well, once we get to those kids and prove they are being held here against their will," said Gladius.

The team split into smaller groups to check each floor of the compound. The massive ziggurat-styled building had four large levels. Each one was made up of a few different floors. Each of the Espada agents took a team of Guild agents and searched a different section. Claymore took a team up to the top section, Katana took the next level, and Dart took the second level. Lastly, Gladius's team continued checking the ground floor.

Although Serena was almost completely spent, she tried to push out with her mind to locate anyone. However, after a few mental sweeps, she turned to the others and shrugged, uncertainty in her eyes.

"I'm not getting anything," she said. "So, either this building is empty or these walls are designed to keep out any mental probing."

Gladius made a clicking sound with his tongue. "I wouldn't be surprised. He probably has a hidden chamber where he keeps them when they aren't being used."

"So, we find that chamber. Even if I have to tear this place apart!" Gabriel's blood was boiling.

The next several hours were spent looking through each chamber of the energy plant. Serena kept probing the area, but she eventually stopped trying. It seemed useless after a certain point. But still they kept searching. They felt along the walls for any kind of hidden chambers or secret corridors.

To no one's surprise, it was Agent Charm who made the discovery. The teams were now resorting to using earpieces for communication and they got a ping around five that evening. In no time at all, both teams were back together at the bottom level of the plant.

"Did you find it?" asked Zion.

"I think so," Charm said. "I found something odd here. Something told me to check over here, and I found this device that seemed out of place. So, I checked it out, and it was actually a dummy."

"What do you mean?" asked Foundry.

"The device was empty." Charm pulled at a false grate on the side of a machine, and they could see that the entire thing was empty. That is, except for a stairwell that led down under the lab, o the team cautiously went down into the belly of the power plant. The basement was a dim open room. At first, they didn't think anything was inside because it was so quiet. There also didn't appear to be power to the light switches.

"Codex," Serena called into the mic on her earpiece.

"Yes," He was sitting in his work station back at the Espada base.

"Can you access the power grid for the plant? We need lights in the basement."

He paused for a second to pull up the data and then said, "Should be coming on now."

As he said it, the lights to the basement sprang to life. What they saw before them was shocking for even the hardest of agents. There were scores of people in the basement. Most were huddled together for warmth on the far side. Although some were adults, there were many younger teens that were mixed into the group. The oldest minor was maybe sixteen years old. They were dressed in rags, clothes so old and worn that they looked like they would fall apart from a light breeze.

"What in the name of Venus?" Gabriel said to no one in particular.

"This can't be," said Foundry.

Serena rushed down the stairs to the people, using her telepathy to communicate with them. It wasn't a perfect system, but she was able to make them understand that the agents were there to free them. Gladius put his hand on her shoulder.

"I will take it from here," he said. In Spanish, he let the frightened people know that they were from the Espada, an agency of the Protectorate, and here to free them. He apologized for their situation and pledged to make sure that they received the best treatment that was possible.

Gabriel and his team started helping to get the people out of the cold basement and then out of the building. As the people were leaving the building, they saw Sergio as they exited and spat and cursed at him as they passed. Claymore stood by to make sure nothing too extreme happened to him, but he was perfectly fine watching the slaver get covered in spit and dirt.

After the captured people were all freed, they were taken to the Espada headquarters so they could figure out where they were going to be sent. Many of them were from the neighboring towns and cities, but even more were from surrounding countries. A few weren't even from South America.

"So, that means this is part of something bigger?" Gabriel asked as he sat in the headquarters with his team.

"It could be," said Serena.

"We need to get information from these people. We need to see if we can find the people who kidnapped them and sent them here."

"We will," Gladius said, walking up behind him.

"Oh," Gabriel said, somewhat sheepishly. "I uh...didn't realize you were there."

"No problem, amigo. We're all on the same team here. But you're right. This leads us to a new step in the mission. Phase two, if you will. We need to find the people who are kidnapping gifted and sending them here. I don't believe this is an isolated incident."

"Well, let us know if you need anything. We would be happy to help out."

"Indeed. We may just be doing that," he said. He turned to leave and added, "And thank you again."

FILE #11

VENEZUELA

That night, the Guild remained in the on-site sleeping quarters. Every agency had rooms for agents to sleep on the base for situations like this. Oftentimes, agents were on call to help with a situation or they needed to be on standby for a developing situation. So, more times than not, these rooms were filled.

Zion walked around the area, checking in on everyone. As the acting leader of the mission, she wanted to make sure everyone was physically ready. She let them know that they would be debriefing with the Espada agents and then moving on.

Simon and Gabriel bunked in a room with Hardlight and Piledriver. Hardlight brought them some drinks from the break room and they were able to hang out together with some relative peace, which wasn't a common occurrence for the Protectors.

"So, Sentry," said Hardlight. "How do you like being an agent? Is it everything you hoped for?"

"I think so," said Gabriel. "I love what I do. I'm excited to use my gift to help people."

Piledriver laughed. "I just like that we get to fight for a living. Honestly, when I got my gift, I was going to be an Arena fighter. But things didn't pan out."

"Well, we are glad to have you on the team," said Gabriel.

"I'm going to get to bed," said Codex, not quite wanting to get involved in the conversation.

"Yeah," said Hardlight. "Me too."

The following morning, the group was greeted with a large breakfast buffet provided by the Espada. When they arrived in the large breakroom, Gladius told them it was in thanks for helping them solve the mission with minimal problems.

The spread was amazing. Lots of Colombian dishes. Flat cornmeal patties called arepas topped with eggs and cheese, fresh fruit, plantains, and circular pastries called bunuelos. It was all so good that Gabriel couldn't help himself from having seconds and thirds.

As they ate, Gabriel was finally able to ask Gladius a burning question he had. "Hey, Gladius, sir," he said. "I had a question for you."

"Ah," Gladius said. "Sentry, right?"

"Yes," Gabriel said with a smile. "How are the kids from yesterday doing? Are they all right?"

"Oh, of course," he answered. "They are obviously scared and somewhat shocked. But I think they're all hopeful. We're going to be starting the process of sending them to their homes today. Many of them will be back home in a matter of hours, thanks to our teleporters."

Gabriel nodded enthusiastically. "That's good to hear. I am sure they were all a little scared with everything that happened. But I just wanted to ask. Have a good rest of your day."

Gladius then gave Gabriel an unexpected bearhug. As he let him go, he said, "And you as well. Best of luck on the next leg of your journey."

After their meal, the group was led down the hall. Gabriel noticed how similar their base was to the Guild's headquarters.

He wondered if they had a similar contractor or if the Protectorate oversaw the building of the bases for each agency. As they walked, Codex was lost in thought.

"You all right, Codex?" Gabriel asked.

"Oh, sorry," he said, coming out of a daze. "Yes, I'm fine."

Codex was about as good at lying as a two-year-old. Gabriel could tell something was up with him. "What's on your mind?"

"I've just been thinking that something is odd about this mission. I don't understand everything that's going on. It's starting to bug me."

"What do you mean?" Gabriel asked. "This lady went after the Protectorate, so we're going after her. It's that simple. Isn't it?"

"I suppose if you look at it that way. But I think there might be something else going on here."

Codex was unable to elaborate much more than that since they'd arrived at their destination. The Espada agents led them to an upstairs meeting room that reminded Gabriel of the War Room. Codex, though, made note that their system wasn't as efficient as the one he'd set up back home.

"When we get back, you should let me look over your interface. This system could use an overhaul. I mean look at that," he said, pointing to something in the room, but the Espada agent had no idea what he was referring to.

"Yes, thank you," Katana said. "I will let our team lead know." She extricated herself while Codex was looking around the room and pointing out problems with different parts of the room. She sat down next to Zion, giving her an exasperated eye roll.

"Thank you again for volunteering to come with us on this part of the mission," said Zion. "You don't have to know you."

"Oh, I know. You know I have always been a proponent of inter-agency work."

Zion nodded. "That's right. You wrote your dissertation on it in college, right?"

"I sure did," Katana said. "Inter-agency politics can be a headache, and I want to show that our agencies can work together. So, what better way than to practice what I preach."

"Well, we appreciate it. It will be helpful to have someone with us who knows the terrain," added Zion.

As Gabriel collected Codex, who was still finding things to fix in the room, the meeting began. Everyone sat at a circular table so they could see each other as they made up their battle plan. Katana brought up a map of the border between Colombia and Venezuela and showed them the area that they would be sneaking into and the path they would take. It seemed like they had the whole situation planned out.

"So, any questions?" Katana asked before explaining some of the details, like team compositions and Montenegro's involvement. Katana had a contact near the border. She was a smuggler of sorts, but they didn't say much else. They met her in a hotel in a small town near the edge of the country.

Katana booked a room, and they had Nyx teleport everyone inside. That helped them avoid any suspicion, according to Insight when Gabriel asked. He didn't understand why they were sneaking into the hotel room, but she told him that it would be too noticeable if they saw ten agents go into a single hotel room. So, this way we can meet her without drawing any suspicion.

"Nice to meet you," said the woman in the hotel room. She was a short, mousey looking woman with a warm, wizened face with deep laugh lines.

She smiled and greeted everyone by shaking their hands. But Katana got a big hug.

"It's been too long, Katana. How have you been?" she asked.

"I'm good, Janus," she said. "Do you think you can get us in?"

The woman looked puzzled for a moment. "Well, it's a little bit different than my usual work. Usually, I'm trying to get people out of Venezuela."

"Why are people trying to get out of Venezuela?" Gabriel asked.

She looked over at him, her creased face making her eyes disappear. At first, Gabriel braced himself for a verbal bashing or worse. He gritted his teeth ready for the tongue lashing when instead, she put her hand on his shoulder.

"Unfortunately, the government of Venezuela has devolved into a dictatorship that has made it difficult for the people to live there."

"I knew it was bad, but why doesn't anyone do something? Can't the Protectorate help?"

Katana interjected. "It's sad to say this, but no. The Protectorate has jurisdiction over gifted cases alone. It would be seen as a power grab or something worse, if the Protectorate tried to step in."

Gabriel hung his head, disheartened, but Janus picked up his chin and looked into his eyes with her tiny eyes. "Don't worry, friend. I know one day, the people will be free." He smiled as she turned to the others. "Well, let's get this thing moving. I don't have all day, you know."

She spun her hands around into a circle, rotating several times until a large vortex appeared in the space ahead of them. The circular portal showed a large open barn that looked like it had seen better days. Katana didn't hesitate as she was already walking through the portal. Zion followed her with Insight on her heels. The others followed and were on the other side of the portal. The air went from cool and regulated in the hotel to a balmy, sticky mess in the barn.

"Are we in the rainforest?" asked DarkSky, dabbing his forehead with a pocket square.

"More or less," she said.

"So, is this where you get the refugees out?" asked Gabriel.

"Something like that."

Katana turned to the far door, walked over, and peeked through the slit in between. Once she was satisfied, she turned back and nodded. "We're clear," she said.

She and Zion opened the doors. Outside they saw a run-down farm with a broken-down tractor and some overgrown fields. Serena looked around to get an idea of where they were. She touched the tractor, but to her surprise the dust didn't come off. It was painted to look old and rusted. Now she understood. Best she could tell, this place was made to look old and abandoned. They probably wanted it that way so the authorities wouldn't suspect anything and then they could use the place to get people wherever they needed to go. They didn't call her Insight for nothing.

FILE #12

At Dawn, We Monitor

The team found themselves walking down an old mining path that had long been abandoned. From what they'd been told, most of what made Venezuela such a powerful country was its rich mining resources. The country practically cornered the metal market for everything from smartphones to jewelry. However, when the gifted came onto the scene, some were able to create those very same metals and it led to some hostility with the Venezuelan government, which probably led to their lack of communication with the Protectorate.

According to Janus, they were going to come to an old mining town that was still operated by Montenegro. They would need to find a place to hide out there. Fortunately, they were able to make good time and got to the village before nightfall. They could see the village from the top of the hill they were on.

"We'll camp here tonight. In the morning, Hardlight and DarkSky will go down into the village and see if you can find us a room to rent for the next few days if we need. Then we'll teleport into the room so we can set up an operation base," said Zion.

So, they spent that evening camping under the stars. It was a beautiful scene. A crystal-clear lake reflecting the starry night was absolutely breathtaking.

Gabriel gasped in awe. *To think, we were on the brink of destroying the planet before the gifted came around. If they hadn't been able to pivot to clean energy and other conservation efforts, beautiful vistas like this would have been a thing of the past.* He'd never seen such a wonder in all his life.

That night, they all took turns keeping watch in pairs so they could make sure everyone stayed awake. Things were a little too dangerous to risk it. When Gabriel was woken up, he was paired up with Codex and took his post at a tree outside of camp. Codex was transfixed on the smartphone on his lap. That meant he was using it to communicate with someone.

A moment later, Codex looked over. "I was just checking in with Insomnia."

To this day, Gabriel wished he'd caught himself, but unfortunately, he replied, "Man, why isn't he asleep?"

Codex looked at him blankly. Gabriel just held up a hand as if to say, *don't bother*.

"You do know that Insomnia's gift is the ability to survive without sleep, right?"

"I know. It just sort of slipped out."

"Well, anyway, he wants to talk to you," Codex said.

Gabriel's eyes widened and he pointed at himself in disbelief. Codex nodded and handed him the phone. Gabriel took the phone. "Hello?"

"Sentry," said Insomnia, his thick Irish accent coming through the line. "How are things?"

"Good so far. No issues on our end."

"That's what I like to hear. So, as you know, I'm fielding this mission from here. Just overseeing things. I wanted to just touch base with a real person, since the human computer didn't have much to say," said Insomnia.

Gabriel rolled his eyes. He didn't quite like the jab at Codex. Just because Simon was more interested in computers than people didn't make him a bad guy.

"What do you want to know?" Gabriel replied in a somewhat icy tone.

"Well, I need some updates on your position and such," said Insomnia.

"We're overlooking the village. It's called Vista Noche. Tomorrow we're going to start staking out the place for Montenegro and Astrid."

"Good, good, good, laddie. Let's see. What else?"

Gabriel updated him on everything else that had gone on over the last day or so, and soon, Insomnia said he had what he needed. He told Gabriel and Codex to keep communication to a minimum from this point on and only in extreme circumstances because they were close to Astrid, and they didn't want to give their position away.

Insomnia hung up somewhat abruptly. Gabriel looked at the phone as if he wasn't sure what just happened.

Back at base, Insomnia then started his report on the mission, logging everything that had transpired so far. He looked over at his cane and picked it up. About three years ago, he had almost lost the use of his legs during a mission in Drake's lab against a foe called Zero. After it, he'd been stuck in a wheelchair, but he had been able to progress in his physical therapy. He made the transition to crutches, and now he was just using a cane. Although he had made good progress, he wasn't back to his old self yet. Despite being a man with more time than the average person, he still wasn't able to make the process go much faster. His body, although it didn't need sleep, didn't have the ability to speed up the healing process.

If only I had a physical-based gift, I might have recovered by now. Maybe I would have even been able to help in that fight with Zero.

But there was no sense dwelling on the past. He planted the cane on the ground and stood up. With a few shaky steps, he started moving. Once he got going, his legs started to get the idea, and he moved smoothly. He stopped at the window and looked outside at the track. He would usually do a work out session at this time of night. Sometimes he would even practice a sport. Before the incident, he had been getting pretty good at American Basketball. A strange game, he thought. He grew up on rugby and football. What the Americans called soccer was his favorite sport, and he was quite good at it. It helped that he could literally practice twice as much as the average person.

After some depressing thoughts, he turned around and got back to filling out his report.

Before long, morning was upon the team. They were up and ready to move the moment the sun broke over the edge of the horizon. As planned, Hardlight and DarkSky went into town dressed as civilians. They went into the nearby hotel, which was extremely high end for a small town like this. Despite the modest village, the hotel stuck out like a massive monolith in a desert. It had large white pillars in the front with a rather modern look. The stone side was made of polished marble.

Inside, the black tile stood as a deep contrast to the white walls and polished counters. They walked along the wide foyer to the front desk. There Hardlight asked if they had an availability for large suites on the top floor in flawless Spanish. Although the dialect was a little bit different, as Hardlight was of Mexican descent, the words were understood.

The hotel manager was able to get them a large suite with a perfect view of the whole town. When they went up to their room, the two agents quickly checked the room for any unusual additions to the room. However, after they scanned it for mechanical listening devices or any signs of tracking, they felt like they were good to give the rest of the team the go ahead.

As they were doing so, Insight was back in the field listening into their minds. Once she heard them reach out to say they were ready, she looked over to Agent Nyx. "They are ready for us," she said.

Nyx looked at her phone. Hardlight had sent her a live feed of the room. There was a large open wall that would be perfect for a shadow portal, so she focused her mind on that location and summoned a shadow. One by one, the team walked into the darkness. Gabriel stepped into shadow and stepped out into one of the most elegant rooms he'd ever visited before.

Immediately, the team began preparing themselves for their next phase. Now that they were in Montenegro territory, they would begin a long stakeout to keep an eye out for the sale. Odds were that Astrid would be on her way here now, if she wasn't in the village already. Most of the team was certain that she was already there. Gabriel was tasked with helping Codex get his workstation set up. He put up cameras to help them monitor the surrounding area, this way they wouldn't have any blind spots.

Gabriel and Nyx were also able to sneak onto the roof to set up some caroms for Codex. When they returned, Hardlight was leaving.

"Everything all right?" Gabriel asked.

"Zion wants me to get a lay of the land," he replied. "So, I'm going to go look around the town and see if I can find any leads on our suspect."

"Need any help?"

"No, I'm good, Sentry. Boss wants me to go solo. Less suspicious that way."

Deep down, Gabriel didn't like the idea of a teammate being on their own. In his soccer days, they had stressed teamwork. Now this was his team. He didn't want to leave a team member on their own. As Hardlight walked off, Gabriel wondered if he should ask Zion to reconsider her plan, but then he mentally sighed. Zion wasn't known for her ability to listen to other ideas. She had a hard nose if ever there was one.

In the other room, Gabriel found Codex still setting up his small workstation. Because they were mobile, Codex was working on a very paired-down version of his normal computer setup. A fact that he was complaining about as Gabriel entered.

"How am I going to work with a setup this small?" he asked Gabriel.

"I mean, you can communicate with the technology in your mind, so do you really even need a monitor?"

Codex stopped and looked at him. "I'm going to pretend you didn't say that." Then he quickly got back to setting up his smartphone, which was acting as his monitor. They worked together to get the system up and running.

Nyx sat back and watched. Gabriel wasn't helping much other than to reach the places that Codex couldn't. It was like Codex knew exactly what was plugged into what despite the jumble of cords and plugs that were around him.

Sometime that evening, everyone was called into the large bedroom where Zion had set up her office. When they arrived in the large room, they saw a wounded Hardlight. Zion and Serena were cleaning him up. Gabriel walked over to check the severity of the wounds.

"What happened, Hardlight?" he asked.

"I got into it with some thugs in town. They heard me asking about Montenegro," he said as Serena put alcohol on his eyebrow. He winced, which caused him to pause. "So, they said that they knew something. They said to meet them in the alley behind the bodega. So, I walked out, and they tried to get the jump on me."

"Oh man. Are you all right?"

"What did you learn?" Zion asked, more concerned about his mission.

"Well, I took out the first couple, but they had some backup. So, I took them out as well, but I kept one conscious."

"Did you use your gift?"

"No, I did it the old fashion way," Hardlight answered.

Zion nodded approvingly. In these situations, gifts gave them the advantage, but they'd also stand out. Especially something as flashy as Hardlight's gift. "Foundry, take Insight and do a mind modification, or wipe if you need to, on our friends behind the tavern. Why don't you take DarkSky as well?"

The crowd returned their attention to Hardlight. "So, what did he say?" someone said.

"They said they didn't work directly for Montenegro. They're like second- or third-tier underlings, working for the guys that work for Montenegro or something like that. Anyway, they said that tomorrow Montenegro is going to be having some big party to celebrate the good year. But word is that this is a cover so Astrid and other bad guys can come over without much suspicion."

"So, the party is a cover?" asked Zion. He nodded. "Did they say when the party would begin?"

Hardlight shook his head and told them as much as he could, but he eventually needed to rest. The team met for a quick overview after he left the room. Hardlight's information would be invaluable, because now they had a time and place. Gabriel watched as Codex pulled a menu on his phone, then he cast the device to the hotel television. It was a thin screen on the wall, but it was large enough for everyone to see the entire thing. Fortunately, Codex was able to make every device in the room work for him.

"So, I will set up here, in this water tower," said Codex. "It looks over the wall of the compound that Hardlight told us about."

He brought up a satellite view of the village and panned out to the east of the town. He zoomed in. One click, two clicks, three. On the screen, they could see a large compound. It was a full-on mansion that seemed to be a set with a full platoon of guards. It was a strange mix of lavish extravagance and military protection. There was a massive pool with camouflaged patrols. Beside a crew of security officers was a buffet table topped with meats and cheeses and fruits.

"Is that a golf course behind it?" asked DarkSky.

"Indeed," said Zion.

Just then Foundry, DarkSky, and Serena came back.

"What'd we miss?" Serena asked.

"Just taking a look at the compound now. Seems there is a party tomorrow that I am assuming we will need to get invited to. This is where the sale will be happening tomorrow," said Codex.

Zion asked how the mission went. Insight told them that she muddled with their memories just enough to make them think they were beat up by multiple people, none of which looked like Hardlight. Sentry nodded. Although it would be impossible to completely modify their memories, Insight had been able to give them some false ones to make it difficult enough for anyone to pick out Hardlight and compromise their mission.

Codex then resumed his directions. "So, I'll need someone with me to act as backup, while the remainder of the team acts as a forward team to engage once we have eyes on Astrid."

Zion looked over at Serena. "I assume you will be on the observation side, and DarkSky, why don't you work from there. You can offer us cover with some fog if we need and even blast them from range." He nodded reluctantly, but it did make sense.

Serena, however, was a little bit more combative. "Do you think I could be up front this time?"

"Negative. We need you protected this time. You're too valuable to have close to the front lines."

Codex showed them another area on the map. "There's a great staging area here. Nyx could teleport our people into the dropzone here."

"So, Nyx, you wait in the water tower as well with the observation team. When you see the exchange going down, I want you to open a portal for us to engage the targets."

Nyx nodded.

Zion looked around at her team. "All right, team, let's get some rest. We begin monitoring at dawn."

FILE #13

THE PARTY

The following morning, the team was up at the crack of dawn. Zion was up first, readying everyone. Codex was set to man the video feeds and had tapped into the town's security feeds on top of their own. Any business security, traffic, or dashboard cameras were fair game for him. He was even able to tap into Montenegro's cameras, which there were plenty. This gave him nearly limitless access to the goings on around the compound. He set up an algorithm to hack into the camera whenever anything came within close enough contact to it. Hopefully, this would give them immediate confirmation when Astrid and her team would be nearing the exchange.

Meanwhile, Gabriel and the away team were readying to strike. Although the party would be that night, they wanted to stay ready just in case. For all they knew the exchange would be first thing in the morning or a week from now. So, they would begin their reconnaissance immediately.

Nyx got the observation team to the water tower without being seen, but it was DarkSky who gave them enough fog cover to get inside without anyone noticing. Serena and Codex set up their workstations so they could monitor the compound.

'Why don't you take a rest, Nyx," said Codex. "You need to be ready later on when things get interesting."

Nyx sat down in the back. It was rather spacious, albeit with a rather musty smell. It had obviously been out of use for some time now, but decades of holding stagnant water had left their mark.

"DarkSky, do you think you could get some air flowing in here?" Nyx asked as she laid down.

"Sure." He opened the hatch at the bottom and at the top and made the air swirl through the whole structure, greatly improving their nasal situation. It wasn't perfect, but it was much better.

"Need any help?" Serena asked, looking at Codex.

"Not right now. I've set up my cameras on a pretty high-end algorithm. They'll alert me if anything goes on."

"What are you doing then?"

He looked at her. She was pointing to another tablet that was running some kind of program. The screen has code and a diagram she had never seen before moving around on it.

Codex looked away for a moment, and then he returned his attention to the tablet. "I've been wondering what is going on with this whole Protectorate attack. Something seems odd to me. It doesn't quite add up, so I'm running a program to try and find what information they stole." He looked up at the completion bar.

"Looks like it is almost finished."

"Not quite. Should be a few hours. Maybe more because this is a pretty intense bit of decoding. But then I need to analyze the data because this system I made is just making it so I can check the data."

"Why don't you do it personally?" she asked.

"Because I have to be here to monitor the cameras and make this whole system run. This setup wouldn't run without my gift," he said very matter-of-factly.

Time passed slowly for the team. The first hour came with no real change. The second actually saw some action, but it was mostly catering companies and party supplies. However, this meant they had to monitor and identify each and every person that came and went. They were all watching for any odd behavior that might signal that the deal was happening now.

Around noon, Montenegro came out onto the back patio and went for a swim. He was a rather portly fellow with a haircut that looked like it was from a generation long since passed. One that hadn't been in good taste even then. He was wearing the largest aviator sunglasses anyone had ever seen. After a rather short swim, he lounged by the pool for a few more hours. Then he finally got up and went inside.

"'Join the Protectorate,' they said. 'You'll protect the world from all kinds of villains and evil,' they said. No one mentioned watching a large man lounge poolside for hours as one of the things I would have to endure," Serena complained.

"This is brutal," said DarkSky.

Finally, Codex received a blimp on one of his cameras. A vehicle was approaching the compound for the first time all day. It seemed that the villagers kept away from the compound unless they were expressly ordered to do so.

"We have a bogie," said Codex. The rest of the team approached the screen. On screen was a plain black van that was somewhat nicer than the other ones in the town. It pulled up to the main gate. The driver pressed the key code. A few seconds later the large iron bars opened and the car entered the compound.

Codex nodded at Serena. "Give them the go ahead."

Serena turned around and focused her mind. *"Zion, we believe we have the sellers."*

"Good," said Zion. *"We are ready to engage. Let us know the moment we have verification that the sale is going down."*

"Copy," Serena said.

They watched another car pull up to the gates. However, when this driver lowered the car window, it was an older man.

The car entered the compound as they monitored. Several more started pulling up at the gate.

"So much for the party just being a cover." She quickly reconnected her mental link to the team. *"Team, it looks like the party is a real thing. We should move to infiltrate the party."*

Zion answered back, her voice was strong and loud. Insight wondered if Zion's psychic-type gift meant that she had a stronger mental connection. *"All right team, let's move to that plan. Insight and Nyx, you two need to get our people into the party. You know your jobs."*

Foundry, Charm, and Gabriel had already been chosen as the infiltrators. Charm was the obvious choice to use her gift to find the meeting and get them to their target. Foundry was actually quite good at infiltration, and her gift lent itself to being able to protect herself. Gabriel, on the other hand, was chosen because he fit the build for a run of the mill bodyguard. As Zion put it, "Your nondescript features make you pretty unremarkable, so you will blend in well."

He wasn't sure she'd meant it as an insult. In fact, she probably was trying to compliment him in her own weird way, but it didn't come across well. But he didn't have any unusual facial features, and he was also pretty average in size and weight so she did have a point.

"Nyx, tell us when you're ready. The away team is in position," Zion said.

Nyx watched the guests approaching the main gate. She needed to find a spot to teleport them into the parking area, close enough to not be noticed but far enough away to not be suspicious. This would be a bit of a challenge.

There was a car parked to the far side, as if the driver hadn't wanted their vehicle near the others. They were already gone, but there was a lull in the parking on that side.

"All right, ready in three, two, one."

Foundry, Charm, and Sentry all fell into the shadows and held their breath. In an instant, they were behind a large black vehicle. It was definitely a custom vehicle, because nowadays, cars weren't designed to be this bulky. It probably had special plating and blast-resistant glass.

"Someone's expecting an attack?" whispered Gabriel.

"Probably just a thug who is used to working with unsavory people," said Foundry.

"Shhh," said Charm. "We need to get moving."

She looked around the corner and saw the coast was clear, so they all stood up and walked away from the car. Fortunately for them, their standard suits would fit in a setting like this. Most of the other attendees were in flashier three-piece suits and lavish ballgowns. One woman was wearing a massive hat, and another was wearing an ornate mask. The people here certainly had a unique sense of style.

The three got into position, with Charm and Foundry taking the lead. Foundry put her arm out and Charm locked hers around it. Gabriel walked behind them like he was their bodyguard. Realizing they had their earpieces in, he discreetly put his hand up to Foundry's ear like he was whispering to her. He quickly plucked the earpiece out, and tucked it into his pocket. He did the same thing to Charm.

Now, Serena would be their sole source of communication, which wouldn't be a problem since they were a safe distance away. Over that link, Foundry said, "Nice job, kid."

Gabriel smiled for a split second, but then he remembered where he was. He quickly schooled his expression into a serious mask of determination. He set his jaw and narrowed his eyes, trying to look tough. Personally, he thought he was nailing it, but it came across as a little off putting.

The three were approaching the main door. "Insight, you're on," said Charm.

Serena zoomed the camera in on the two guards at the front. The two guards were holding small tablets with a checklist pulled up on the screens. She waited to see which one would be checking them in. It would be tricky to get past both of them so she really hoped that only one of them would check them in. It looked like the one on the left would be checking them. That guard was tall and lanky with a stern expression and her eyes were a malevolent red color. When Foundry and Charm came to the front of the line, she asked for their names.

"Lady Bubbles and Queen Lizard Teeth with their bodyguard Goldendoodle," said Foundry.

The guard looked at her tablet for the names. Although the name wasn't there, Serena tricked her mind into thinking it was. "All right, go on in."

The three walked in, trying to hide their smiles. *"Nice work,"* Gabriel said in his mind. *"We could have said any name and that would have worked, huh?"*

"Yup," Serena replied.

"Nice."

Once inside, the three looked around. Immediately, their training told them to check the exits and find possible means of escape. "We have a large balcony on the second floor to the east," said Foundry.

"There are also a few French windows on the front wall," Gabriel said. "And we have a large exit at the back that leads into the courtyard."

Then Foundry said, "I'm seeing multiple guards posted on interior balconies. In total, I am counting ten."

"I see them," Gabriel said. With their mental link, he knew exactly which ones she was talking about since he could see them too.

Now that they had that out of the way, it was up to Charm to find Astrid and the meeting. They both walked around, trying to look like casual guests. Gabriel couldn't help but feel like everyone was looking at him. This part of the job wasn't his specialty. If it wasn't for his defensive gifts, someone else would have probably been chosen for this part.

"No sign of Astrid yet," said Charm. "She isn't here yet."

So, they pretended to mingle as best they could for the next half of an hour. Finally, Charm's ears perked up. She looked around the room to see Astrid entering at that very second. "She's here," she said to the team.

"I'm watching her." Foundry was on the second floor and could see much of the party, including the entrance.

Gabriel was being dragged off by a cheeky English woman who wanted to dance. He was making his way back inside when he got the call. He entered in time to see Astrid walking through the foyer and into the main portion of the mansion. She snaked around to the staircase, went up the stairs to the second floor, and then to the third floor.

"Foundry, are you tailing her?" Charm asked.

"I got her," said Foundry. "Sentry, make your way up to the third floor. Use the other staircase."

"Got it."

"But keep your distance. We don't want to tip her off."

FILE #14

DECODING THE DRIVE

Codex's program was finished so he looked over the small screen at the data. It was a jumble of code, completely encrypted. Completely useless as is. For anyone but him. He dove into the computer, his subconscious speaking with the computer program as he looked at the program's code.

"Can you show me what this code means?" he asked.

"You do not have access to this information."

"Yes, I do," he said.

"Confirmed," the program answered, believing his statement.

"Can you show me the information?" Codex asked.

"I don't believe I can tell you."

"You can tell me."

As if given the password, the program changed its mind. It decrypted the code and then showed Codex a list of names. So many names. Countless people. But for some reason, most of the information was inactive. Why was this information like this? He dove deeper into the program, his mind so entranced that he was no longer thinking about the mission.

He looked at the list of names again. All of these agents, so many of them. What did they all have in common? Instantly, he sorted by all the common categories he could think of. Nationality, gifts, mission roles, and on and on. But none of that seemed to be a common factor. So, what did these agents all have in common? Some were rogues on stealth missions, while others were your standard brutes with no stealth missions at all. Others were intelligence-gathering agents with no combat training. There didn't seem to be any trend or common aspect that they shared.

Then something hit him. He was scanning the list again, this time looking at their careers, and running multiple program searches through the countless agent's files, looking for any common or repeated terms.

Finally, he noticed something. The agent was deceased. How could he have missed that. He was so dead-set on finding something kind of career or gift related commonality, that he completely missed that. Quickly, he reconfigured his search parameters, this time sorting by those that were deceased.

Just like that, he found what they all had in common. All of these agents were dead. He ran another quick search. These agents all died in the field. Well, they were all supposedly dead. Then he saw Astrid's name on this list. If she was on this list, and these were agents they believed to be dead, could more of these agents have been mislabeled? He pulled up the picture of the agents that were with Astrid at the attack on the Protectorate a few days ago. As he feared, there were two matches.

"Agent Surge. Birth name: Dillon Reese," Codex read while looking at the still from the security footage and Reese's standard issue agency identification picture. It was only a ninety-three percent match, but he was clearly the same guy. Although the angles were different, there was enough of a match for it to be impossible to be someone else. From what Codex could tell, Reese was able to generate electromagnetic pulses.

Next, Agent Raven. Birth name: Seneca Morgan. She was there as well. She didn't exhibit any gift outright, but she might be some kind of physically enhanced fighter. "Looks like she can manipulate parts of her body," said Codex. "So, like make her hands into swords or something, I guess."

After quickly scanning their files, Codex was certain. The names on this list were all agents who were suspected to be dead. But were they really?

Then a terrifying thought hit him. If they were all dead agents, why would this list be useful? Who would want to buy a list of agents that were dead, but not really? It didn't make sense.

Codex cut the connection to the computer, and his consciousness came back to the material world around him. He hated that sensation. In the computer world, he was limitless. He could do anything, make anything, be anything. But in the physical world, he was trapped in a weak, undersized body. He shook his head. Now wasn't the time to think about that. He looked over to Serena. She had barely moved. He checked his watch. Although it had seemed like hours to him, in real time, it had been seconds, almost a minute.

"I think we have a problem," said Codex.

"What's wrong?" asked Serena.

"I finally decoded the information that was stolen by Astrid," Codex answered. "All of the agents on the list are dead. Or at least suspected to be dead. All were killed on missions."

"You know that could get you into trouble, Codex," said DarkSky.

Codex nodded. "I didn't use the conventional means, so they'll never know."

"Well good. I mean I wouldn't snitch, but I'm glad they won't ever figure it out. *Anyway*," said Serena, dragging out the last syllable to make her point. "What does that mean?"

"I think this means things aren't what they seem. Astrid and her two accomplices are all on the list of agents that were KIA, killed in action. So, I'm wondering what that could mean," Codex said.

"So, if this list has agents that are dead, but she's on the list and she is clearly alive, this list isn't exactly accurate. Therefore, it's not exactly a valuable thing, right?"

"That's what I'm trying to figure out. How can they sell a list that's incorrect?"

DarkSky groaned. "So, break it down for someone who isn't as smart as you two."

"I think this is a setup. I think there is no sale."

Insight nodded. "Let me contact Zion right away."

Insight turned to focus her mind once again, but just as she did, the water tower lurched. The ground shook and everything tilted. From the monitor, they could see that Montenegro's guards were standing in a cluster, and one of them was holding her hands out to the tower. She fired a blast of energy from her body and struck the tower. Somehow, the enemies knew that the agents were inside the water tower.

"We are—" The tower started to shake and she lost her connection when her focus shifted. Her survival instincts took over. There was another massive shift, then the whole water tower shook. Seconds later, the water tower slammed into the ground.

Gabriel's group was still following Astrid as she continued walking to the top floor of the mansion. Gabriel kept walking past guests, and he could have sworn that their eyes flicked to him every time. Was he just paranoid? He was starting to think that he didn't have the mental fortitude for this. He was refocusing his attention on the target when he heard metal screeching and then a loud crash outside. He was about to turn to the window when several guests stepped in front of him.

From his position, he could see the water tower crashing down to the ground. The guests all stepped forward, cutting him off from getting outside.

"We have a situation," came the voice. It was in his ear, not his head. Their mental link was down. Of course it was down, Serena was inside that water tower. How could he be so foolish to not realize it? He needed to get to her. He needed to figure out what was going on here.

"I think this was a setup," Foundry spoke through his earpiece. "The party guests aren't guests. This is a trap. Get out now!"

Gabriel turned around. He needed to get Charm out of here. One of the guests bull-rushed him, slamming him into the guard rail. Kneeing the guard, he kicked him off. Two more blasted him with concussive blasts, but Gabriel was quicker. He shielded himself and threw all of them back into the wall.

Just then, a massive metal vase flew through the air and slammed into the three guards that were sneaking up on him while he was distractedly scanning the grounds for Charm. Gabriel turned to see Foundry smirking. She was taking on her own set of enemies, yet, somehow, still keeping an eye on him.

Energy blasts came at her from all angles. People on the lower floors were shooting and even more people were rushing up the stairs. Gabriel and Foundry had several guards between them. She didn't know what to do. A heavyset man and two shorter women approached, grabbing at her. From a distance, they all were pulled back as if by invisible strings. They slammed into the ground, and Gabriel jumped over them. Landing next to her, he picked her up.

"We need to get out of here," he said.

"No kidding," she said. "How do we do that?"

"Not sure," he said. "Where is the nearest exit?"

Charm looked around for a moment to get her bearings. "Follow me."

She started running the way that he came. There was a balcony that led outside across the way. Gabriel saw several guards reach the top of the staircase. He pushed forward with his telekinesis and slammed into the first ones. They fell back into the others behind them on the staircase, causing a ripple effect and all of them fell back down the stairs. A few were able to off energy attacks before they tumbled down. One even was on target, but Sentry was able to block it.

"We need to get out of here!" Charm glared at him in annoyance as she ran.

"I know that!" Sentry wasn't far behind her. "I'm just playing defense."

As they approached the balcony, three of the partygoers jumped up from the lower floor. The first rushed at Charm, but Sentry pushed her back with a powerful surge of telekinesis. The second teleported behind Charm and grabbed her. Charm elbowed him in the face and then kicked him into the wall. Gabriel finished off the third one, leaving them room to make it to the balcony.

Charm rushed through the glass doors first while Gabriel paused to look behind them. Foundry ran for the opposite side toward the other balcony. She pulled the metal railing and used it as a weapon to slam through the guards as she weaved her way through them like a snake. Her control was impressive. She could control multiple pieces at once. That was a skill Gabriel hadn't quite mastered. He wished he was as technical as she was. His strength lay more in raw power.

She made it to the doors, slamming the metal through them and running through without even slowing down. A second later, she was completely out of sight. Gabriel nodded. His team was out of the building and now he needed to get to the observation team. Codex, Insight, DarkSky and Nyx could be hurt. They could be surrounded right now, kidnapped, or worse. He hurried out onto the balcony in the cool darkness of the night.

FILE #15

HER REAL MISSION

On the other side of the battlefield, Astrid watched with Montenegro. The plan was going perfectly so far. She would have what she came for, and the Guild would be dealt a devastating blow. She flicked her eyes to the portly man. His shirt was buttoned far too low and showed off way too much chest hair evn though he thought he was pulling it off. But no one should ever wear their shirt like that. Ever. At this point, the shirt was barely even serving a purpose. She rolled her eyes. He would have to be dealt with in the end. He knew too much. He had seen her, and he knew her motivations. No one was allowed to be aware of such things. She'd let Morgan do that.

Her attention returned to the battlefield. "Things are going according to plan."

Montenegro, with his big booming voice, said, "Indeed. Our partnership has yielded a bountiful harvest. We are like two cranes flying in the wind. Nothing can touch us."

She stifled the urge to vomit. He was such a windbag, she thought. But he was necessary at this point. "Indeed, it would seem. We are going to need to keep as many as we can alive. Your men know that right?"

"Yes, we are aware of that. Plan A is in effect. My men are the best. They would never disobey a direct order. They're like my cubs, and I'm their papa bear. They love me. They worship me. I have given them life to the fullest."

Once again, she needed to keep from rolling her eyes. A simple yes would have sufficed. She turned. "Well, then I suppose they won't mind me joining them on the battlefield. I need to find what I came here for anyway."

Montenegro swallowed audibly. He hoped his men would follow orders. Despite the praise, they were little more than poorly trained gifted. They were like children with scissors really. Dangerous and inexperienced. He sighed.

In the distance, Gabriel could see the wreckage of the water tower. He would need to make his way in that direction. However, something gave him pause. Zion had already reamed him out once on this mission for leaving his position, but in the end, she did admit it was the right thing to do. Well, she never said that, but Gabriel had gotten the point.

Montenegro's troops were all over the place. This mission had quickly turned on its side. This had been a setup from the beginning. That was obvious at this point. The enemy somehow knew they would be in the area watching and waiting. It all made sense. Otherwise the sale probably would have happened much sooner. They wouldn't have waited several days. They would have gotten rid of it sooner and disappeared into the wind. But instead, they had waited for the Guild to get here. They probably had their own surveillance watching them as they watched Montenegro.

Gabriel had lost Foundry when they'd exited the building, but she had made her way back around all on her own. Now she was deflecting incoming attacks with two large, spinning pieces of metal. They looked like what were once the hoods from two different cars. She must have ended up in the parking lot, which was perfect. Beams of energy, fireballs, lightning blasts, and more soared through the air. It was just like fighting at the ziggurat.

Just then, Zion landed beside Gabriel as he deflected an attack from the blaster across the lawn.

"We need to get a team to recover Insight and the observation team," said Zion.

He nodded. "I will take point."

"Good. Foundry and I will lead the counter attack here. You take Charm and go find Serena."

Sentry nodded again and moved back. Charm had moved back behind the others as they moved into position, helping direct the others. Gabriel ran up beside her and gave her the reassignment. She nodded and said, "Well, you know that means you are doing all of the heavy lifting."

He nodded. Charm wasn't a combatant in the field, but she excelled in other ways. Her ability to locate objects and generally get lucky made her a very useful teammate. Still, if a powerful gifted came at them, Gabriel wouldn't have much help dealing with them. Although, she had handled herself well in the mansion.

As they ran, Charm glanced over at Gabriel. *Could he be a loyal agent?* The day that she was assigned to this mission, she had received a call from her boss. Not the agency. Not the Guild. Dexter Romulus. He was the high-ranking Protectorate official who had contacted her to act as an informant for him a few years ago. So, ever since then, she had been sending him information on missions, agents, and anything else that might be important. To her, most of it seemed like basic Protector and agency stuff, but she wasn't being paid to ask questions, just to pass along details.

The day she was contacted, she had been in her office. Her special phone, the one he had given her, rang. It could only call and receive calls from one number, and only she could use. If anyone else tried to use it, the phone would activate its failsafe and become completely unusable. It also had a single app on it—not a game or your usual social media app, but one specifically designed to work against a very specific person. Codex. The app made the phone invisible to his abnormally perceptive mind when it came to technology. He wouldn't notice this device even if it was in the same room as him. At least, that was what she'd been told, but she had no intention of testing that theory.

"Sir?" she asked as she picked up the phone.

"Hello, Agent Charm. I hear your agency was tasked with going after the person responsible for the attack on the Protectorate," Mr. Romulus said.

"Yes sir."

"Very good to hear. I know your agency will do us proud."

She could hear something in his tone. He was unusually cheery. Normally these discussions were more formal. There wasn't this false pretense. It sounded odd to her. Maybe he was just being polite, so she let it go.

"Oh, well, yes, sir. I hope our agency can do you proud."

"Did you get on the team?" Romulus asked.

"Yes, I did," she said. "We leave shortly."

"Where is the rest of the team?"

"They're gearing up. But I was already in uniform, so I ducked out of the meeting to check my office. I thought you might be calling."

"You're a perceptive one, Charm. That's why you have been tasked with this mission."

She was uniquely gifted. Hers was an unusual and even unexplainable gift. It made her incredibly useful. Although even she didn't know exactly how to explain it, she knew that it was an important gift.

"Usual mission parameters?" she asked.

"Yes, we still want you to monitor the other agents and give us any updates you can on the mission as you go about your usual duties. However…" He paused. There was a sense of tension in the air, as if he didn't know what to say next. "I want you to inform me when you make contact with Astrid."

"Astrid?" That was odd. Romulus never wanted information on their suspects. It was always information on the agents or the leaders, who was going on what missions, and any oddities in behavior. She was never asked to do anything like this before. For a moment, she wondered what was different about this mission. But that wasn't her call. She wasn't in charge.

"Yes, Astrid. I was in the building when she attacked, so I have a vested interest in her capture. So, if you make contact do your best to let me know. Understand?"

She swallowed hard. She never questioned orders before, and she kicked herself for even giving a hint of doing so now. "Yes sir. Forgive me. I wasn't questioning your orders. I was just caught off guard—"

Romulus cut her off. "No, that's fine, Charm. You are a good soldier. Forgive me. I am just upset over this attack. Continue your mission. Your family is enjoying the payments."

She sighed. As part of their arrangement, Charm was having money sent back to her family in China. They were very poor, and Charm already did her best to support them. When her gift developed, she'd used it as an opportunity to get into the Protectorate Academy and get out of poverty. Ever since then, she enjoyed the finer things in life. But she always tried to support her family as well.

"Thank you, sir," she said.

Just then there was an explosion nearby, and Charm was brought back to the present. She shook her head as if to shake the memories out of her head. She knew better than to focus on something other than the mission at hand. But now that Astrid was on site, she would need to contact Romulus immediately.

"Have you found them yet?" asked Gabriel.

She shook her head. "No, but I think we should go this way."

She focused her mind as they moved in the general area of the wreckage of the water tower. But they weren't headed right for it. Something in her gut told her that they were not directly at the scene. When they came to the wall, Gabriel pulled them both up in the air and over it. They landed on the other side and then kept running. Right across the street was the water tower. But they ran past it, and Gabriel tried to stop.

"Why aren't we stopping?" he asked.

"They aren't here, Sentry."

"But..."

She was still running and didn't stop at the wreckage, so Gabriel kept following her. He didn't quite understand her power, but even he knew that she was almost always right in these situations. So, they rounded the corner, and there they found their missing team.

"Everyone all right?" Gabriel asked.

"We're fine. Nyx got us out just in time," said Serena.

Gabriel gave her a look. Although DarkSky had started talking, he kept his eyes on her. Even though things weren't good, it was helpful to know she was all right.

"The rest of you stay here," DarkSky said. "Sentry and I are going to engage. Insight, keep us posted." He took to the air. Gabriel wasn't nearly that good at levitating himself with his telekinesis, so he stayed on the ground. Levitation made him somewhat nauseated because of how unsteady it was. He ran, jumping over the debris with a telekinetic push, which allowed him to clear normally impossible heights. He cleared several cars that were in the way. When he came to the wall, he pushed himself up over the wall and landed back in the battlefield.

Meanwhile, Charm was looking around for a place to be alone. She needed to contact Romulus, but there were the other agents right there. It would be too suspicious to take a call in front of them, and it would be even more suspicious to leave. She would need some kind of distraction.

Just then, Serena dropped to the ground. Nyx grabbed her, and Codex helped her sit up.

"What's wrong?" Nyx asked.

"My head hurts...I think I bummed it before we teleported."

"Here, take it easy. You could have a concussion."

Charm smiled. *Perfect.*

FILE #16

THE RAVEN

At first, the battle looked like a fair fight. The agents were able to hold their own in combat. However, the real difference was the sheer number of guards that Montenegro brought to the fight. Even when they fought against the guards in Colombia, the numbers weren't this one-sided. They were being overrun.

Gabriel and DarkSky entered the fight, bringing some needed manpower to the battle. Zion looked over her shoulder and smiled when she saw them.

"About time you brought some firepower."

"This doesn't look good," Gabriel said.

"It isn't. Somehow she knew we were here. Somehow Astrid set up this ambush."

"Why don't we just run?" asked DarkSky.

Gabriel would never admit it, and he would never say it, but he was wondering the same thing.

"Our mission is to get Astrid. Even if we're ambushed, we need to complete the mission. Not for the Guild, but for the Protectorate as a whole. All of those agents could be in danger," Zion said.

"Then, let's go get her."

Foundry was ahead of them and saw them coming from behind. "About time you joined us, Sentry. I was worried you decided to pack it up."

"Not a chance," Gabriel said. "Besides, someone has to help you out."

"Oh, believe me," she said. "I can handle myself."

"Don't I know it!"

"Wrecking ball," said Zion.

Taking his cue, Gabriel surrounded himself in telekinetic energy and slammed through the guards ahead of them. It wasn't his favorite move because of the huge drain on his energy, but it was effective. Zion was right on his heels, slashing and dicing anyone he missed. She jumped over him when he stopped and then threw two of her psionic daggers at a guard who was sneaking up on him.

Five guards appeared behind them and then seven more to their right. More and more kept appearing out of thin air.

"This is bad. We have a teleporter on the field who is moving the troops around," said Zion.

"Foundry and I'll take the front," said Gabriel.

Zion moved in behind them while DarkSky took to the air and brought down a lightning strike on the first group. The five guards either scattered or were blasted. Foundry and Gabriel absorbed the attacks from the second group, giving Zion a chance to sneak in and attack from behind. She felled all seven of them before they even knew what hit them.

Then the next group moved in. Gabriel deflected a barrage of energy blasts, but Zion was hit by one. She went flying backwards and landed on the ground, leaving a small indentation behind her. Luckily, she had been able to create a shield under her, cushioning the blow. She shook her head as she stood up, mentally kicking herself for allowing herself to be hit.

Not again. She summoned two long swords in her hands. Now, it was time to make them pay. A fiendish smile appeared at the corner of her lips. It was dangerous work. But someone had to do it.

Energy attacks exploded around her. She bobbed and weaved as she ran toward the attackers. Most of them were untrained. They all probably had a basic understanding of their blaster gift, but nothing more than that. They didn't know how to aim well and didn't know how to take environmental factors into account. Most of them aimed like their ability came out of their eyes, but they were using their arms as sights, so they never quite landed where they wanted. She shook her head.

How did I let one of these hit me? she asked herself. *Well, even a broken clock is right twice a day.*

They'd gotten lucky before, but she was going to make them pay for that. She ran a wide circle around them, causing some on the far side to accidentally blast their allies. There was some confusion and they didn't recover. She dropped them all with a few precise strikes. Gabriel joined her moments later. He had just dispatched the other group of guards. They moved back-to-back, keeping an eye on their surroundings.

"We're getting killed out here! We need to find the teleporter!" he said.

"I doubt they are on the battlefield," Zion said.

"So, how do we get to Astrid?"

On the far side of the battlefield, Hardlight was holding his own from a distance. He and Piledriver moved to the right of the open field. Piledriver was taking on the hand-to-hand combat while Hardlight fought from a distance. From where he was, he could see DarkSky flying overhead, dropping down thunderous strikes of lightning on the Venezuelan thugs. He smirked. This would be one for the books. It seemed they were going to win.

However, he didn't notice the woman coming up behind them. She slammed through the other guards and bulldozed Piledriver. She grabbed his legs and slammed him into the ground like a shovel. She turned to face Hardlight. It was the woman from the attack. Not the shadow wielding one, but one of her accomplices. From the video, they hadn't been able to tell if she was even gifted or just an incredible fighter.

Piledriver stood up. "Where are you going?" he asked the woman.

She turned around, almost shocked. "Well, well, well. You're a tenacious one."

Piledriver patted his exceptionally large shoulders. "I'm just built tougher than most."

"Let's put that to the test!" yelled Morgan.

As she rushed Piledriver, she held out a fist. Piledriver wasn't afraid. His body could take almost any amount of punishment. However, just as she approached, her body shifted. Her fist morphed into a metal wrecking ball and slammed into him. He stumbled backward, and she jumped on him.

She kicked and punched him while he was on the ground. Hardlight froze, looking on in shock and horror. The brutality of it all gave him pause. For a moment, he didn't know what to do. But then, he snapped out of it and summoned his power. Light shimmered around him and small spears of pure light formed. He shot them out at Morgan.

A bone-like exoskeleton appeared around her, protecting her from the light spears. They slammed into the earth, deflecting off her tough outer shell. Hardlight couldn't get to her. *What in the world is her gift?*

She had transformed her arm into a large metal ball and she created a bone shield on her back. Was she able to somehow morph her body or something?

Morgan finally stood, leaving Piledriver in a broken heap on the ground. She turned to face Hardlight. "You know, my people used to tell stories about a god-like being called Raven. He was a trickster god of sorts. He would turn into other animals and people. He would cause mischief and mayhem wherever he went. But he usually did the right thing in the end."

Hardlight swallowed. She approached him almost causally as if as there wasn't a battle raging around them. She walked with the measured steps of someone walking down their sidewalk to grab the morning paper.

"So, what does that mean?" he asked.

"My codename. It was Raven. I took it as a way of honoring my native heritage. It seemed fitting."

"You were a Protector? You were an agent?"

"Yes, but that was long, long ago. Before my agency decided to trade my life for a younger model. I was expendable."

Hardlight stood there in shock. "Why are you telling me all of this?"

Morgan—or Raven, he wasn't sure—continued walking toward him. Hardlight was frozen in a mix of fear and uncertainty. Her hand shifted again. This time, it turned into a blade. Her body was impossible. Her other hand turned into something like a hammer or a battering ram before morphing back into normal hands—well nearly normal. They had bone spikes protruding out of them like brass knuckles.

"I don't expect to let you live long enough to tell anyone any of this."

His eyes widened.

She motioned him closer, as if to say, *Bring it on*.

Hardlight looked down at his hands. He was going to have to fight her. It was do or die. There was no one else around them, and Piledriver was either dead or incapacitated. It was up to Hardlight to stop her. So, he steeled his nerves, summoning every ounce of power he could Small blades of light spun around him and then shot out at her. Many missed, but a few were on target. Like before, she created a bone shield around her arms and his light blades ricocheted off her bone armor.

While deflecting his attacks, she rushed him. Before Hardlight could counter, she delivered a thundering kidney shot, followed by a knee to the gut. His eyes widened as he coughed. He would have dropped to the ground, but she grabbed his collar and punched him again and again. Once she'd decided her brutal assault was over, she threw him to the ground.

He tried to pick himself up, but she was on him again before he could, punching him across the face and breaking his nose. She picked him up by the throat. His feet barely touched the ground. She was surprisingly strong for her size. It was like he weighed nothing.

"I can control every section, every muscle of my body. I can make my bones shift and my skin harden. You didn't really ever stand a chance, kid."

She threw him to the side and he hit a parked sports car from Montenegro's collection, smashing into the windshield. He rolled over the side and fell behind it with a groan. Morgan jumped onto the hood and looked down at him. Her body began to morph once again. Hardlight stared at her with wide eyes, lips quivering in fear.

"How, how, how?" was all he could say. Then everything went black.

FILE #17

According to Plan

Gabriel was blocking energy blasts from almost every direction, almost completely drained. "We can't hold this for much longer!" he called over his earpiece.

They were facing worse odds than they had during the ziggurat fight without Serena's mental link or Espada's backup. Things were quickly turning worse and worse. Zion was falling back now. She looked over to him. "I know. We need to consider an exit strategy."

Despite her desire to fight to the death, things were obviously not looking good for them. She was actually starting to see the writing on the wall. They would have to retreat or she would risk losing her team. However, as she watched, Zion noticed something. Even though they had the tactical disadvantage, they weren't being pressed too hard. Somehow their enemy wasn't overwhelming them like they should have been.

"What is their play here?" she whispered to herself while dodging attacks and countering others. *They aren't trying to kill us? Maybe they're after something else.*

From across the way, Astrid was scanning the field, frustratedly glancing from left to right. Their target was nowhere to be seen. She held her hand up as a massive explosion tore the ground about twenty feet away. She rolled her eyes. Montenegro's troops were barely better than a child with a piece of dynamite. They were going to get someone killed.

"Ma'am we don't see any sign of the target. I'm starting to think—" said a voice into her earpiece.

"We continue with Plan A," she interrupted.

"Yes, ma'am."

She shook her head. The target had to be here. It was the only thing that made sense. She switched her earpiece to a secure channel, one just used by her small team. "Morgan. Begin Plan D."

"Already on it."

More energy exploded around Zion. She risked a glance behind her, shielding her face. Again, their shots were wild. Were they missing on purpose? Poor shots? Or something else?

Gabriel deflected a blast that would have hit Katana. She was busy using her telekinesis to levitate six different short blades around herself. Although he probably should have been focusing on the attack, he was definitely thinking that her gift was cool. Even though they both technically had the same gift, they manifested in different ways. She was much more dextrous with her gift than he was. He struggled with such delicate movements and control. He specialized in shielding and defense.

Just as another group of troops teleported behind them, Katana sliced them up with her floating daggers.

DarkSky was hit by a percussion blast and dropped to the ground. He landed shakily, having a hard time regaining his bearings. With his ears ringing, he planted a leg, and tried to stand but immediately dropped to his knees. While holding up his shield as best he could, Gabriel ran over to his distressed teammate.

"Hey, I got you, buddy," he said.

"Thanks, Sentry," DarkSky said back.

"Can you move?" he asked.

DarkSky shook his head. "I think whatever got me is messing with my balance. I can barely see straight."

Gabriel then turned away. He could see the team scrambling, trying to hold their own as forces teleported in around them. They were outmatched and now fighting a losing battle. In that moment, Gabriel was more conflicted than he had ever been in his life. He never wanted to turn and run. He was not the sort to admit defeat. But if they didn't do something quickly, they were going to lose their whole team. Everyone was going to be killed.

"Nyx, we need evac now!" Gabriel called into his earpiece.

Zion looked back at him with a mix of annoyance and acceptance. She kicked the guard in front of her, threw a psychic dagger at him, and then summoned a large tower shield. A large, glowing, aqua-colored shield appeared in her arms, covering the entire length of her body. She positioned herself to be a defender as Foundry and Gabriel tried to cover every angle. Nyx teleported out of the shadows between them.

Hardlight rushed over to them. "We need to get out of here!" He was holding his side and half carrying half dragging Piledriver.

"Can you help us defend while Nyx gets us out of here?" asked Gabriel.

"No...I think I'm too wounded."

Gabriel didn't see any blood or major wounds on him, but maybe whatever he was dealing with wasn't as apparent. He glanced up at Nyx. "Let's get out of here."

Zion covered one side of the team while Foundry and Gabriel defended the rest of the circle. They were being blasted from all sides now.

"What happened to Piledriver?" asked Zion.

"We were attacked. I don't think he's breathing!" Hardlight yelled, setting him down on the ground. "I think he's dead..."

"What?" Zion gripped her weapon tighter as her anger grew. "How is that possible?"

"I don't know, but whoever took him out was way stronger than we expected."

Piledriver was practically indestructible. *How could someone have killed him?* Shaking her head, she forced herself to look away from her dead teammate. She couldn't dwell on something she couldn't change. She had to focus on her team. She had to focus on getting them to safety. She looked at Nyx, who was getting herself ready to teleport them all away.

"Any time now," said Gabriel.

"Yeah, we're dying out here." Foundry, who was usually unflappable, was struggling to keep his voice steady.

"I'm working on it. I need to line this up right or we could end up falling on our heads," said Nyx. She paused for a few moments. The wait felt like hours to everyone else. Then she finally said, "All right, let's go."

With a surge of energy, Nyx created a shadow portal underneath them. They fell through the ground and disappeared, the energy blasts and projectiles aimed at them crashing into the ground where they had been moments ago.

The team reappeared in the hotel room, which Nyx had prepared beforehand.

"Nice job, Nyx," said Zion. "Good call prepping this room before the mission.

"If I've learned one thing as a protector, it's to prepare for anything and everything. All right, I'm going to grab the observation team. Everyone, clear out of here."

"You got it." Gabriel was helping Hardlight carry Piledriver.

"And make sure you close the door. I need it dark in here."

The rest of the team cleared out of the dark bedroom. Hardlight and Gabriel brought Piledriver to the couch and laid him down. Neither of them had much medical training, but they knew the basics. They checked for a heartbeat and a pulse.

After a few anxious moments, they looked back at Zion. She was watching them from a far corner. Hardlight solemnly shook his head.

Zion turned and punched the wall.

Katana came over to her. "We can mourn the dead later," she said. "We should get the rest to a safe house first."

Although wrought with emotions, Zion was levelheaded enough to know that Katana was right. "Where do you suggest we go?" she asked, her jaw tight.

"The same place we used to get here. I'll contact Janus again, and we'll get out of here. Sound good?"

Zion nodded. Shortly after, Nyx returned with the rest of the team. Serena, Codex, and Charm walked through the door and immediately saw Piledriver on the couch. Gabriel and Hardlight were sitting motionless, staring at the body. Serena sighed. They had lost a teammate, and they had failed their mission.

"Nyx, we need you to get us to the extraction point. Remember the barn we teleported to before?" asked Zion.

"Yes," she said. "But why not just go directly to the Espada base? Or our base, for that matter?"

Katana interjected. "Operational protocols dictate that in the case of a mission failure like this, we need to remain in a safe house or another secure location for twenty-four hours and make sure we are not being followed. If an enemy could find one of our bases, we could be attacked."

Nyx nodded. She shouldn't have questioned their orders. "Yes, ma'am. I'm sorry."

"No apologies needed. Just get us out of here" Zion turned to the rest of the team. "Everyone, get your stuff and let's get out of here."

So, the team quickly packed their bags and acquired their gear. Most of packing up invovled collecting Codex's observation gear. Everyone else had packed incredibly light. In no time, they were all packed.

Gabriel and Codex came back inside with the last of Codex's gear. "I think we're set," said Codex.

"Then let's go," said Zion.

Nyx opened the shadow portal in the same bedroom as before, and they walked through it. On the other side, they found themselves in an old barn. It looked as though they were the only ones there since last time. Katana rushed to the door and looked around.

"All right, no one is here. Everyone, form up and follow me," she said.

So, the team got in line and readied to leave. Although some thought they would remain at the barn, Katana led them through rough terrain to what looked like an underground bunker built directly into the side of a hill. The entrance was covered by what appeared to be a large stone. However, when she was able to move it with ease, they realized it was fake.

Inside, they found a large common area. One that appeared too big for the space provided.

"Wow, it's pretty big in here," said Gabriel.

Katana pointed around the open common room. "In there we have sleeping quarters. There's a small medical room over there, and we have a small kitchen down here."

"So, we should be set to hide here for the time being," said Zion.

Back at the compound, one of the guards ran up to Montenegro. Panting, she struggled to speak. "The agents escaped, sir."

Montenegro's eyes narrowed. He turned to Astrid, who was standing in the corner. "Did you hear that?" he asked, his voice shaking with anger. "This is not what we planned."

She turned to him, hiding her annoyance as best she could. "The deal was never one that you could deliver on, Montenegro." She smirked.

"Why are you smiling?" he asked, somewhat annoyed that she was amused at a time like this.

She turned toward the battlefield and looked at the wreckage that had once been a beautiful landscape.

"Because everything is going according to plan."

FILE #18

TWO AGENTS

Inside the bunker, the team decided to rest for the time being. Gabriel and DarkSky carried Piledriver to the medical room. There was a special roll-out table against the wall for deceased agents. The rest of the team entered behind them. There was an awkward moment, while everyone stood there either looking at the ground or expectantly at each other.

"Would anyone like to say a few words?" Zion finally asked.

No one spoke up immediately, so Gabriel cleared his throat. "I can say something."

As he thought of something to say, he realized that almost everyone else in the room had known Agent Piledriver better than he had. *This is going to be so awkward...* He bit his lip. Everyone's eyes were on him. *Well, here goes...*

"Piledriver was an incredibly strong agent. He put his mission above everything else. He was a true warrior. Although he wanted to become a fighter, I'm glad his path landed him on our team. We were all blessed to have met him and to see him grow as a fighter. I think we all learned something from his no-nonsense attitude and his sense of self. Sometimes I wish I was more like him. I wish I could better convey what I'm thinking..." Gabriel sighed.

He paused for a moment, a lump forming in his throat. He swallowed and composed himself.

"Piledriver, thank you for your sacrifice. We aren't going to let your death go unavenged. You will be given justice, fellow agent of the Protectorate. You truly were a protector. And your memory will go on."

Silence fell over the room when he finished. Everyone patted him on the back as one by one, they trickled out of the medical wing, eager to accomplish whatever tasks they'd been given. Charm was helping Serena up out of her seat.

"Hey, are you all right?" Gabriel asked.

"I worry she might have a concussion," Charm answered. "She's showing some of the symptoms."

"Let's get her on the gurney and start concussion protocols. Here, let me help you," Gabriel said.

Charm and Gabriel helped her onto the gurney. "I think I'm all right, I just bumped my head when the water tower was hit. I just need some rest."

"Well, it'll be safer if we administer the safety protocols, just in case," Charm said.

While Serena received some medical attention, the rest of the team was in the bedroom. Zion was sitting on one of the small, metal bunkbeds. Codex was sitting by his laptop on the far wall, while Foundry, Hardlight, and DarkSky sat nearby.

"So, we are pretty certain this whole thing was a setup," she said.

"Yes, ma'am," said Codex.

"You're telling me that this woman attacked the Protectorate headquarters all to lure us into an ambush?" Zion's emotion was evident on her face. Her eyes were practically bulging.

"I don't think I can speak to her motivations or mindset, however, the facts are that the drive wasn't what we thought it was. Also, there wasn't a sale." Codex paused. "I think Astrid wants revenge on Ein, and she wanted to lure him out into a position where she could finish him off."

"But Ein wasn't there?" DarkSky said.

"A fact that I think threw a wrench into her plans," Codex said.

"So, she expected Ein to be there, and she wanted to take him out," said Hardlight. "Makes sense to me."

Codex nodded. "I believe so."

"But what about that drive?" asked Foundry. "I still feel like there's more there than what we're seeing."

Hardlight gave her a quizzical look.

She shrugged. "I'm just curious."

"I think you may be correct, Foundry," said Codex. "I think the fact that Astrid, Reese, and Morgan are all on that list means these names aren't exactly as unimportant as we may think."

Hardlight interjected. "But what about her plan to kill Ein? Isn't that the priority here?"

Codex nodded "Yes, you do have a point there. We should focus on how to protect the Guild's leader."

"Well, the plan is to stay put for the time being. When we get back to the base tomorrow, we will debrief Ein then," said Zion.

"But if we know there's an active threat on his life, shouldn't we go back to the base now?"

There was a pause as the team considered the proposal. Although it made perfect sense, protocols were protocols. Zion was the one to point that out. She reminded them that because of the situation, they needed to remain here. "If we are being tracked, the enemy team could follow us right to Ein. Tomorrow, we will teleport to the Espada base, and then we will go on to our base. Hopefully, that way we can't be tracked."

There was no way to be completely sure no one could track them.

Gifts were so unique and powerful that no one could be completely sure they were in the clear. It seemed like every day there was a new gift or ability that they had never seen before.

Something that broke the mold for what they believed was possible.

"So, do we have any other questions?" asked Codex.

No one spoke up, so Zion said, "Now that we know the plan, we will rest up here. Charm and anyone else that can, help the injured agents. We have a lot of wounded people to look after."

So, the next few hours were spent taking care of the wounded. Almost everyone was hurt in some way, shape, or form. DarkSky and Charm, who were mostly unharmed, helped clean cuts and stitch up wounds.

Gabriel went to find Hardlight and Zion to see if they needed medical attention. He found the young man sitting in his bed. "You want us to check you out in the medical room?" he asked.

"Oh, no, I'm just tired, but I'm fine otherwise," said Hardlight.

"You sure?"

"Yeah, I think I'm going to go to bed, actually."

"All right. Have you seen Zion?"

Hardlight rolled over. "Check the kitchen."

Gabriel went to the small kitchenette that was attached to the common room. There he found Zion. "Ma'am, it's your turn in the medical wing."

She shook her head. "No, I'm fine."

Gabriel could see several blast marks on her suit and a few even revealed burn marks underneath. "Ma'am, I can see you have a few burn marks. Charm could clean those up for you in just a few seconds."

Zion glared at him with fire in her eyes. "I'm fine."

"But Zion, if you were hit hard enough for it to puncture your protective suit, you should probably be looked at"

For a few awkward seconds, she stood there. He sat down on the chair nearby.

"I hate hospitals too," he said. "When I was a kid, I had asthma. Nothing too bad, honestly, but I had to go in for checkups every once in a while, and I hated it. But fortunately, I was active enough that it never got too bad. I was able to lead a really normal child-hood. But I still don't like going to the hospital."

Zion fixed him with a stern gaze. Her lips were pressed together in a thin line and her jaw was set. Gabriel just sat there in the silence for several long minutes. He was hoping she would open up, but he didn't want to force it.

Finally, after several long moments of silence, she spoke up. "It was my boyfriend. That's why I hate going to hospitals."

Gabriel was almost as shocked as he was relieved. He didn't speak. He just listened.

"I was already an agent when we met. We started dating. I was a different person then. I was happier and kinder, I think. But then I found out that he was a spy. He was working me to get information about the Guild. When he attacked me, I had to defend myself. In the end, I was the one who brought him to the hospital."

She paused for a moment, tears welling in her eyes.

"I stayed at the hospital all night. In the morning, they came down to tell me that he didn't make it. I had killed him. Yes, I know, it was self-defense, but it doesn't change the fact that I killed the only person I ever really loved."

When Gabriel was about to say something, she pushed past him toward the medical room.

"Fine, let's get this over with."

After Gabriel had left his room, Hardlight went to the small lavatory. It was one of the most compact rooms in the hideout. There was a toilet, shower, and sink all in the same few feet of space. He looked around before entering and then quietly made his way inside the room. When the door was locked behind him, his body shifted and altered its shape, changing from the young Hispanic man to a tall, darkhaired woman. She turned and looked at her reflection in the mirror.

Man, that takes a lot of energy.

Morgan, noticing that her suit was a little baggy now that she was in her original form, pulled her phone out of her pocket. It was in multiple pieces, but she easily reassembled it and then she grabbed another device—a small metal encryptor. It was a new piece of technology meant to keep technopathy from intercepting their messages.

She put the phone to her ear, but then paused. She realized this bathroom wouldn't be the right place to talk to Astrid, so she would need to text her.

So, she typed in the number.

Morgan: *Astrid, I am inside a bunker with the other agents.*

Astrid: *Give me an update.*

Morgan: *It will be difficult to complete the mission as the bunker is locked down, and I will have no way to escape.*

Astrid: *Options?*

Morgan: *The agents plan on returning to base tomorrow. So, I will attempt to make the grab when we return.*

Astrid: No.

Morgan looked at the reply. What did that mean?

Astrid: *Instead, get to the base with them, and send us your coordinates. We will join you. I want to be there for the big reveal.*

Morgan nodded. *Yes, ma'am. I will send you the coordinates when we arrive and I will help you get inside.*

Astrid: *Good. Contact me when you are ready.*

Morgan put the phone down and looked at herself in the mirror. She realized she would need to go back in looking like Hardlight. She blew out a long, deep sigh and then readied herself for the very draining task of impersonating Hardlight once again.

The suit filled out once again as she took on his likeness. Hardlight's face stared back at her from the mirror.

Then, she quickly disassembled the phone and put the pieces in her suit jacket. She walked out of the lavatory, ready for the next stage of her mission: infiltration of the Guild.

FILE #19

Mission Failure

Gabriel spent the entire night with Serena in the medical room. Although he dozed off a few times, he tried to stay awake as much as he could to keep an eye on her. They had her hooked up to a machine to monitor her vitals.

At roughly three in the morning, Gabriel felt something in his hair. His head up as he was abruptly pulled out of his slumber. "Wha.."

"It's just me silly," she said.

"Oh, hey. Are you feeling all right?"

"I think so. My headache feels like it's going away, but it's still faint."

"That's good."

"Could you get me some water?"

"Of course." He grabbed a bottle from a stash in the miniature refrigerator in the corner. She took a long sip from the bottle, almost completely draining it and then handed it back to him.

"Have you been here this whole time?"

"Yeah," he said, looking away with a red face.

"You're sweet. Thank you for keeping an eye out for me. I appreciate it."

"Of course," he said. "Anytime."

She held out her hand, and he took it. She rubbed her thumb against the back of his hand. They remained that way, silently looking at each other. Then Serena finally said, "Do you think life will ever calm down enough for us to have some time together that isn't on a life-or-death mission?"

Gabriel made an exaggerated sigh. "You know, I really don't know. I think that's the job. I'm just glad we end up on mission together once in a while."

"Yeah, but more times than not, we're on opposite assignments. You end up doing protective and combat missions, while they usually send me on more reconnaissance missions than anything."

Gabriel looked down, fearing what she was getting at. *Please don't be that...*

"Maybe we can go on a real-life date after all of this, alright?" she said.

Feeling like he could finally breathe, he looked up. "Yeah, I would like that."

"Good." She let go of his hand. "I'm going to get some more rest before the morning. Hopefully when I wake up, I'll be feeling better."

"Sounds good. I'll be right here."

Gabriel sat back down on the chair next to her medical bed. He leaned back onto the bed with his hands crossed in front of him. Serena rolled over, turning away from him. She closed her eyes. A tear fell down her cheek.

Hardlight was up at dawn. The impersonator had slept for a few hours in the lavatory so she could actually rest. It would have been impossible for Morgan to fall asleep in the bunkbeds with everyone else because she would've unconsciously reverted back to her true form. That would have made things more complicated. She sat in the corner, watching them as they slept.

Zion slept right by the door. She seemed to have a deep seeded lack of trust. She would be the one Morgan would need to watch. Then there was DarkSky. He was also one to watch out for. He seemed to be something of her unofficial right hand man. But he didn't seem as untrusting. Then there was Codex. He seemed too smart for his own good. Plus, his natural gift with technology would make him a danger.

Part of her wanted to just off some of these agents while they slept and see what happened. Maybe she could take out one of them, then point the blame at another one.

She shook her head, realizing how foolish that could be. Yes, she could eliminate one of her potential enemies, but she would also make everyone suspect a traitor among them. With the telepath incapacitated for the time being, she had been able to blend into the team with little to no trouble. As long as she didn't do anything to blow her cover, she was in the clear.

A few minutes later, Zion woke up. She looked rough. There were dark circles under her eyes. She turned and saw Hardlight sitting in the darkness.

"What are you doing up?" she asked.

"Couldn't sleep," was all Morgan said.

"Yeah," Zion said, getting up to wash her face.

Before long, the rest of the team was awake. After receiving a fairly plain but highly nutritious breakfast bar that was full of protein and other minerals—according to Codex—those that needed it had their wounds checked. Once again, Morgan refused any treatment. She wanted to stay as far away from that telepath as she could. Just in case.

Around lunchtime, they started to pack and get ready for their departure. Katana summoned Janus to teleport them out of Venezuela. After an hour of waiting in the barn, she appeared. Morgan did her best to stop twitching, but she was very anxious to get out of this body and back to her original form. Plus, the fact that their target was so close that she could taste it made the anticipation almost unbearable.

Janus teleported them out of Venezuela and they reappeared inside the Espada headquarters. Morgan would need to remember this person. Apparently, she wasn't an agent, but she did some contract work for them. Did she work for other groups that weren't agencies? Maybe she was willing to bend the rules a little bit if she was willing to sneak protectorate agents into Venezuela.

Now that they were at Espada, they were kept in a secure room for a few hours where they were screened and swept for any kind of tracking devices. Fortunately, it was all technology-based, and they didn't use anything that would pick up on Morgan. After they were given some food, they were allowed to leave.

"It's been twenty-four hours, team," said Zion. "Let's head home."

So, the team met back up in the teleportation hub and were teleported home. Everyone breathed a huge sigh of relief after they appeared inside their own teleportation hub. Finally they were home. However, their sense of relief soon evaporated. Ein and Trei were both standing there with their arms crossed. Neither looked happy. No pat on the back or congratulations were in store for the team today. Quite the contrary.

Immediately, the entire team was escorted by other agents to the debriefing room, a paired-down and simplified version of the War Room. It had less of the bells and whistles, because mostly it was just for post-mission meetings. As the team was ushered into the room, the guards remained outside. Trei stopped and leaned against the door while Ein went to the front of the room.

To say he looked upset would be an understatement. In the short time that Gabriel had known him, he had never seen Ein look like this. Usually, he was composed and collected. Maybe he was upset because Astrid was still trying to kill him and the team had failed to capture her.

"Well, which one of you wants to be the one that gives me the bad news?"

Zion stood up before anyone else had a chance and gave Ein the full mission breakdown. She explained everything they did from how they worked with the Espada, how they followed a very discrete system, to the unfortunate turn of events at the mansion.

The whole time Agent Insomnia took notes, filling out some of the paperwork for their mission. Ever since the injury he'd sustained during the Zero incident, he had been given a lot more paperwork to do. Because he couldn't do quite as much, he sort of threw himself into his work. He completed about three times the paperwork as the usual clerical employee, mostly because he never slept and worked around the clock these days.

Once Zion had finished her explanation, Ein remained silent for a few moments. Everyone watched and waited, unsure of what he was about to say. Ein had a practiced poker face. His facial expression could either be the beginnings of a tirade or a thoughtful contemplation. It was impossible to tell which. His stern expression was practically impossible to read without some sort of mindreading or extrasensory perception. Something Gabriel didn't have.

"In all my time as an operations leader for the Protectorate, I have never seen a mission so clearly boggled. We're going to be a laughing stock! You walked directly into a trap!"

Ah, the verbal tirade, Gabriel thought. *Here it comes.*

"Sir, our team followed all mission protocols and went by the book on this. But Astrid clearly knows our agency's systems and protocols. She knew exactly how we would handle this and where to go. But we won't fail again," said Zion.

"There won't be a next time. You are all relieved from this mission. Head back to your offices and finalize your reports. We will be sending a new team after her immediately."

Zion made to offer another protest, but Ein shut her down. Zion stormed off with a cloud over her head. Once out of sight, Zion punched the wall in frustration. The rest trickled out of the room. Some left quickly, with their tails between their legs, while others stayed behind to speak with captains. Insight was collected by Captain Ivy, who needed to speak with her and

Charm. Gabriel and Foundry went to their wing to fill out their paperwork. Eventually everyone went off to compelte their work, everyone but Morgan. She made for another part of the Guild headquarters.

Unknown to the rest of the Guild, Astrid's team was waiting just outside of view. From an office building's roof, they watched and waited. They had two high powered telescopic lenses trained on the Guild's headquarters. Few knew the real purpose of the building. But now, Astrid knew the location of the Guild. She could finally get what she came for.

Each member of her team was an outcast. Each of them was also a reject from the Protectorate. They were her most trusted colleagues. Like her, they were ones who saw the problems with the Protectorate and she realized she wanted to give them all the information. They didn't know exactly what they were fighting for. She needed to tell them exactly what this mission was about.

She looked over at Yui and Reese. Her eyes were somewhat downcast as they all sat there together, readying themselves for the next step. Reese was watching through one of the lenses, keeping an eye on the target and taking notes. Meanwhile, Yui was beside him, watching through the other lens, calculating her jump. She would be the one to teleport them into the building, so she was preparing herself.

"Team," Astrid finally said. "I need to tell you what this mission is really about."

Yui looked over, confused. "We aren't going to be taking out Ein?"

"Well, if that happens, it'll be a happy coincidence. What we're really after is my daughter."

"Your daughter?"

"Yes, she's an agent in the Guild. She, however, doesn't know that I'm her mother."

"Who's your daughter?"

FILE #20

The Other Mission

Jake took off his suit jacket and hung it on the chair. They were using an apartment across the street from the cultists. Crimson was watching a group through some highly sensitive equipment. They had been following a cult that called themselves the Reapers.

Jin, or Agent Kaze as she was officially called, was stretching.

"So, why does this cult call themselves the Reapers?" Jake asked.

"Didn't you read the mission report?" she replied.

"I mean I skimmed it. But I'm here mostly because Pius is said to be behind this cult."

Kaze nodded. Yes, it was true. Pius, Jake's arch-nemesis was on the loose. He was caught and sent to prison, but he had escaped. Now, their intelligence showed that he was going around starting this highly destructive and volatile groups. Now, several of these groups were turning into cults and deadly terrorist factions, but the agents didn't understand what exactly Pius's goal was.

"This cult said they want to lessen the world's population because they think the world is overpopulated."

Crimson cut them off. "Hey, shut up and listen to this, you two!"

He quickly turned the volume on his listening equipment from his headset to the speakers so they could hear. Once he did, Jake and Jin could hear the cultists's conversation.

"...After we hit the capital, we move onto the big office buildings,"

"But after we destroyed the harbor last week, won't security be kind of tight?"

"It doesn't matter," said a third voice. *"We need to do this. We need to cull the herd. If we don't do something, the world is going to reach a tipping point."*

Jake snapped his fingers, "All right, we have a confession. They're the ones who destroyed the harbor, and they're planning two more attacks."

Jin stood up. "I'm actually with Brimstone on this one too. I say we move in quickly."

Crimson raised one finger and continued to listen further.

"But I think we should seek guidance from our leader, Lord Pius. He should be made aware of the potential attacks, right?"

"After we've succeeded, we can tell him about our good work. He'll be happy about what we're doing. He believes in our cause. He is the one who sparked the fire of our revolution."

Crimson nodded, whispering more to himself than the team."All right, we now have confirmation that Pius is directly involved. But tell us where he is, burn it all!"

He was growing more and more frustrated. They had done so many of these stakeouts, but they still didn't have a confirmed location yet. But it sounded like the meeting was wrapping up.

Crimson quickly stood up and made a spinning motion with his finger. "Let's move team," he said. "Let's grab them."

The three of them rushed up the stairwell to the roof. Because they were on the top floor, it was a quick run for them. Jin was the first to reach the roof, and she quickly grabbed her climbing gear from her side. She sprinted ahead of them, jumping onto the ledge of the building.

Jake stared at her in awe. *Damn, she's fast!* She went from zero to full sprint in a second. She threw one end of the grappling hook onto a standing antenna, hooking it perfectly. Before Jake or Crimson were even in position, Jin jumped off the edge of one building and onto the other one. She cleared the landing with a few feet to spare.

She quickly attached the other end of the hook onto the opposite building. Jake and Crimson quickly repelled across to the other building, while Jin got into position. She climbed down the side of the building, moving like a spider. She reached the window and peered inside to see the cultists preparing to blow the building. This was a low-rent, somewhat run-down apartment building with probably fifty or sixty poor families inside. Jin couldn't let them destroy this building and get away.

While the other two got into position, she leaned over, pivoted, and threw her weight at the glass, smashing through the window. She would have preferred a stealthy entrance, but she needed to react quickly. Hopefully, this entrance would scare them into fleeing instead of blowing up the building.

As she hoped, the cultists reacted to her presence. One screamed, "It's the fascist Protectors!"

Many of them started to flee, but a few of them rushed her. Unfortunately, Jin didn't know which of them were gifted or what abilities they possessed. So, she was going into this fight somewhat blind. The first few all threw wild punches. Jin weaved through them and took them out easily. Another fired a blast of dark red energy at her. She dodged, jumped up over him, and landed behind him, delivering a perfectly placed kick to send him to the ground.

Jin had placed an "Out of Order" sign on the elevator and barricaded the stairwells. The plan was to chase the cultists to the rooftop. There they would find Crimson and Jake waiting for them. Then it would be a simple matter of rounding them up.

Brimstone and Crimson waited on the rooftop. As usual, Brimstone did not like the waiting. His hands repeatedly shaking, repeating the snapping motion he made when he sparked a flame in his hands. Crimson, however, was patiently waiting. He snapped his head over to the younger agent and said, "Here they come."

A second later, they barged through the door. It was a mixed and diverse group of individuals all running in a panic. Jake snapped his fingers, and a flame sparked around his hands. He was on the cultists instantly.

"Brimstone!" Crimson yelled. "Remember, they could be mind-controlled."

One of the cultists punched the young agent in the face while he was distracted and he crashed to the ground. The super-powered hit had almost broken his jaw. Then the cultist kicked him and sent him flying. When Jake landed, he rolled over and glared at Crimson in annoyance. "Yeah, sure. I'll take it easy on them. No problem."

He then delivered a punch and a sweeping kick, knocking the cultist out, and then moved on to take out the others. Crimson found himself facing a gifted able to create explosions. She must have been the one that blew up the harbor, and she would most likely be who destroyed the capital.

Grabbing some small stones from her pocket, she threw them at Crimson. They all exploded around him like small grenades. She peered through the smoke, certain he would be finished.

"You see, sweetie. My gift lets me play a little more reckless than other people." His voice drifted out of the smoke. As it cleared, she watched, stunned, as his wounds healed in a matter of minutes.

With that, he rushed her and knocked her out. Jin was joining them now after having made sure that the halls were clear of the cultists. Before long, the agents had apprehended the rest of them. Crimson looked around and whistled. "Well, we got 'em all."

Jake kept an eye on them while Crimson called the mission in to headquarters. Once that was done, the mission was wrapped up, and they were headed back to their base. Fortunately, for them, Nyx was back on base so she could teleport them back instead of them having to take a vehicle.

"Got to love teleportation," Crimson said as they entered the mission room.

Jake smiled and nodded in agreement. Jin wasn't a great conversationalist, so a car ride with her would have been rather boring. Now that he was back, he wanted to finish up his paperwork quickly. He still hated paperwork, no doubt about it. It was the worst possible thing. As often as he could, he would put it off, and other times he would try to pawn it off on another agent. But that rarely worked, since he was the most junior agent.

He walked up to the operations wing. The Guild was separated into four wings. The intelligence wing, which was overseen by Ivy, The R&D wing, which Duo ran, the combat wing, which was where Trei worked on combat training and battle simulations, and finally the operations wing. Captain V was now the leader of that wing. Jake walked into the large open room, which housed several cubicle-like sections. Agents were filling out reports in a few of them. He and Gabriel were lucky enough to have their desks near each other.

When Jake stopped at his cubicle, he found Gabriel filling out a mission report.

"Brimstone is back!" he announced with a huge grin on his face. However, Gabriel didn't look up. "Everything okay?" Jake asked.

"Uh, not really. Mission did not go well. So, we're benched. Ein said another team will take over for us," Gabriel answered.

"Dang, that sucks."

"No kidding."

"Want to tell me about it?" Jake asked as he sat down to fill out his own paperwork.

"I'll tell you what I can."

FILE #21

EIN

"Welcome to the Guild headquarters." The imposter let Astrid and her team into the building.

"So, this is Ein's temple to his own ego, hmm?" Astrid said, looking around.

They were in one of the backrooms leading into the main building. Morgan looked over at her boss and asked, "So, can I drop the disguise now?"

"You know the plan. Keep it up until we're sure that our cover is blown. Just in case," Astrid said.

Reese led some of their troops to the door. These were some of Astrid's best warriors. Each of them had a number of successful missions under their belt and she'd gladly fight alongside any of them. "You know the plan. Stay in your formations and follow the protocols we gave you. Yui is our extraction plan, so just contact her if you need to leave the building."

While Reese went over the plan with them, Morgan said, "So, she should be in her office with the other intelligence agents filling out their mission reports."

Astrid smiled. "Then that's where I am headed. The rest of you follow the plan, and I will get my daughter out of here."

The team moved off into their respective positions while Astrid made her way to the wing where her daughter was supposed to be. She slammed through the doors, expecting to see her.

Instead, the office room was empty. In fact, the entire intelligence wing had been evacuated. Astrid's gaze darted back and forth, hoping she might find someone she could question. But no one was present. Shadow spikes stabbed through one of the desks as her rage grew, cutting it into pieces.

Composing herself, she brushed back her hair and then smoothed out her blouse and took in a few deep breaths before leaving the wing. She needed to find her daughter. Everything hinged on finding her. She walked down the hall to the debriefing room. Maybe she was still in there after their meeting. It made sense. Maybe she would be speaking with her superiors.

That thought made her sick. Superiors. Like the Protectorate actually was in charge. They were just as bad as the villains and monsters they captured. She was glad to have gotten out. It was also why she was so determined to get her daughter out as well.

Finally, she reached the door and listened carefully. There were voices inside, but she couldn't make them out. Sliding over to the other side, s grabbed the doorknob. Quietly, she pushed the door open and peeked inside. A darkhaired man in a white suit was standing at the front of the room. His suit was somewhat different than the more traditional three-button suits the agents here wore.

Then she saw him. Ein. She pushed the door open and looked at him. Almost immediately, Trei turned around. Thanks to his hyperkinesis—which gave him advanced reaction time—he had picked up on the change in air pressure as soon as the door opened. Ein wasn't looking at either of them. He was too busy checking his email on his phone. His eyes widened when he eventually did look up and saw her. All the color drained from his face. His gaze flicked to Trei for a moment before returning back to her.

Trei was already moving to stand in between them. Although Astrid was an extremely powerful gifted, his warrior's pride wouldn't allow him to walk away. He would die right here defending his comrade if he had to.

"Well, it's been some time, Astrid," Ein said after a moment.

Astrid stood in front of Ein. He looked like a mouse trapped in a cage. No, he was more slippery than a mouse. More like a snake or a frog. She sneered as she approached. He didn't move. Despite his fear, he remained rooted where he stood.

"I see you've been well," he added when she didn't respond.

"No thanks to you," she said.

"You know that if I believed you were alive, I would have done everything in my power to come after you."

"Don't give me that. You didn't care if I was alive or dead. You just wanted to make sure you looked good for the board so you would get a promotion. I was just collateral damage."

"Astrid, you were our best agent. You were not expendable. I was planning on recruiting you when I started my own agency. You were like a daughter to me."

"So, tell me what happened that day then," Astrid said.

Ein's eyes locked onto her. Astrid looked so different now. There were grays in her once completely dark hair. Her face was still etched in that stoic expression, but she looked more weathered now, like she had seen too many hard years. Ein looked down, his heart beating louder and louder. He was certain she could hear it with how quickly it was thumping in his chest. Finally, he looked up at her.

"You know what happened. Our team moved in once we got the go ahead. Everything was green. Then, as we worked on pulling out of the city, we were attacked. We thought we lost you."

As he was talking, memories flooded back to her. The explosions all around her. The heat on her face. Then the utter darkness. For a moment, she was afraid of the darkness. But then she shook off her fear. She was the master of the darkness. The shadows obeyed her every command. When she arose, she hadn't been afraid anymore. She'd taken out scores of terrorists single-handedly, slaughtering them all one by one. Afterwards, she realized that her team had left her. No, Ein had left her. He'd made the call to pull out and leave her behind.

"You didn't even look for me!" she yelled.

"We couldn't risk our whole team," he said. "It was a terrible choice to have to make. I pray no one ever has to make a call like I did. But I had to make a judgement call, and every night I have to live with the consequences."

He paused for a moment and the two stared at each other.

"I know why you're here. So, if you want to take my life, then go ahead and try."

"I'm not here for you," she said. "I am here for my daughter. I'm here to take her away from this place."

For a split second, Ein was completely taken aback. *Her daughter? Who could she be talking about?*

Then it hit him. It made so much sense. How did he not see it before. But he didn't have long to dwell on it. She was still talking, but Ein didn't catch what she had said until her last sentence.

"But I will gladly kill you if the offer stands!"

She dashed toward him. Trei intercepted her. As he jumped into her path, shadow claws sprang from the edges of the room and closed in around Trei. He was able to dodge both of them, but barely. She was quick, much more so than he expected, but no one other than an actual speedster was as quick as Trei.

A shadow spear shot out at him like a dart. He dodged that as well and tried to counter with his own attack, but she kept him at bay. Although, he couldn't get any closer, she wasn't able to hit him. At first, Trei thought that was fine. He would be able to keep her tied up long enough that backup would arrive to swing the tides of battle. However, her assaults became more and more ferocious.

Meanwhile, Gabriel was just finishing up his story. Jake looked at him. He wished he was better at knowing what to say or how to show he cared. "I'm sorry, man. But don't let it get to you. Every agent fails a mission or two. Remember what Coach V used to tell us. Back when he was our coach and not our boss."

Gabriel nodded. In unison, they both said, "You have to have a short memory with your failures."

You couldn't dwell on your shortcomings. You had to focus on the positive, otherwise you would fixate on it too long. Part of Gabriel still had trouble accepting it. That perfectionist side of him hated failure. Although Gabriel knew that he could move past it, he also knew that he would push himself to be better next time.

Just then, there was a loud rumble. The two of them looked at each other, eyes wide with panic. They were both up out of their chairs in seconds, rushing to the source of the sound. "I think they're here!"

"That shadow lady?" asked Jake. "Here? How?"

"I don't know. But she knew everything about us. How we operate and everything. She must have figured out where our base was located."

"This shadow lady sounds terrifying, man."

"I think she's after Ein. We need to find him and keep him safe."

As they moved through the halls, other agents were running in different directions. Gabriel couldn't help but notice how much bigger the Guild had gotten in the last two years. Ever since the Jericho attack with the Titans, more agents had signed on with them.

"Where is Ein now?" asked Jake.

"He was in the debriefing room last I saw…"

Meanwhile, Trei was thinking about how to attack. As it stood, all his gift was allowing him to do right now was dodge attacks. He didn't have his gear—his tactical belt and the two short swords he usually brought into battle—but he did have things in the room. As he dodged, he grabbed a pen, a letter opener, and a pair of scissors from the surrounding tables and desks. *I don't have the room to land a frontal attack. Her defenses are too good for that.* He smiled to himself.

After dodging another attack, he threw the letter opener at the wall. It bounced off at just the right angle and stabbed her in the leg.

She screamed in pain, winced, and then pulled it out. It was just a flesh wound, but it still stung. This time, she would cover her front and rear.

In a fury, she unleashed a blast of shadow energy that shot out in all directions. Trei could barely dodge the attacks. The tables and chairs around him were torn to splinters. The blast tore at the walls like an angry cat. Trei, like he had with the letter opener, bounced the debris off the walls and the ceiling in between her attacks. A stream of jagged debris came flying at her, but at best, it was a distraction.

She surrounded herself with shadow energy. Trei was starting to worry that this might be a losing battle, but he wasn't about to give up. He had run countless missions. He had defeated every single adversary he had come up against. He wasn't going to let this rogue agent defeat him. His pride wouldn't allow it.

FILE #22

CHANGE OF PLANS

Yui was watching a screen from a safe distance. She had gotten a full blueprint of the Guild HQ from Morgan. Small dot moved around it, each one represented her team. However, a few of them were different colors. Those were Morgan, Reese, and Astrid. They were not to be interfered with.

The others, however, were the ones she was focusing on. She thought about how things were going. To her, everything was running lie clockwork. Perfectly timed and executed. Nothing like a perfectly timed plan. She flicked her hair up and smiled inwardly, allowing herself a small moment of satisfaction. But there was work to be done. She refocused on the screen in front of her and tapped on the small circular lights moving on the map of the building, directing several where to go. "All right now you're going to the R&D wing."

The renegade agents teleported into each wing and immediately sprang into action. Over and over again, different agents were blindsided by an attack and then the invaders would disappear just as quickly as they'd arrived. Their plan was to confuse the Guild agents enough to get in, get Astrid's daughter, and be long gone before they knew what hit them.

However, Astrid was still stuck in a grudge match with Trei. Their entire mission hinged on the element of surprise and timing. Both of those were now gone.

Meanwhile, Gabriel and Jake were running through the halls when a woman appeared before them. She wasn't an agent they recognized and she also wasn't in the Guild's standard uniform. She was in combat gear.

Gabriel took a defensive stance while Jake moved to attack. This was their usual dance. The pair were like oil and water, yin and yang, fire and ice, but for some reason, that worked for them. Their differences were what made them effective as a team as well as such good friends.

"I got this!" Jake said. "You get to Ein. He could need your help."

Gabriel nodded and reluctantly ran past them. He didn't like leaving his friends to fend for themselves—it was just his nature—but he knew Jake could handle himself. He rounded the corner, sliding on the waxed floors.

It wasn't long before Gabriel found himself at the debriefing room. Just as he was about to enter, a figure slammed into him. Both of them went flying. Gabriel looked down to see Trei, battered and bruised, and looked up to see Astrid. She didn't look like someone who was overconfident or cocky. She simply had a look of determination on her face.

He took a defensive stance, unsure what she would do. This woman was so much stronger than he was, Gabriel wasn't sure how he could hope to stop her.

"Do you know where Nyx is?" she asked as she stepped out into the hallway, leaving Ein in the room alone.

"What?" he said. "No."

Before he could even think past his confusion, shadow tentacles whipped out at him. They slammed down around him like giant spears, slashing the ground and stabbing the walls.

One of the shadow spikes glanced off to his left, forcing him to move in that direction. He glanced into the room where Astrid had been a few moments ago. Ein was still inside. He was confused. Why wasn't she going after him? Wasn't this all about getting revenge on him? This made no sense. Why would she be fighting Trei and now him, if her target was right there? None of this made any sense.

Astrid just stood there as her shadow attacks sliced the air around him. His telekinetic shield was the only reason he wasn't getting carved up like a piece of meat. *She's so strong!*

"You should leave," she said. "You aren't strong enough to beat me. But I'm not here for you anyway. So, you'd die for nothing."

"I can't do that! You attacked our base. That means you're in the wrong. So, you are going to answer for your crimes."

She laughed. "*My* crimes? You worked for the Protectorate. Do you even know how corrupt it is?"

Gabriel knew all too well what she meant. In fact, he was working with a small team to figure out who was behind the corruption in the Protectorate. But she didn't need to know that.

"There may be things wrong with it, but we're still devoted to helping the world. While you…You're just a killer! You killed my allies! My friends!"

Astrid didn't know who he was talking about, but she was certain someone had died during her first and second attacks. Probably someone he knew and cared about. As much as she didn't like that fact, it was a necessary sacrifice. She would pray later and ask for forgiveness for those deaths.

Despite her talk about letting him leave, her attacks didn't let up. Gabriel wasn't going anywhere. Not even in the face of overwhelming odds like these. Not against an opponent that was leagues and years ahead of him in experience and power. He needed to stop her and figure out what was going on here. He had to bring her down and make her pay for her crimes.

But how? She's so strong, she could probably take on the entire Guild and win!

He looked over at Trei. Before today, Gabriel thought Trei was unstoppable. He'd brought down a ton of the Titans in

Jericho a little over a year ago—single-handedly, by the way—but here she had defeated him by herself.

Just then, Nyx came running around the corner, her shoes clacking against the floor, alerting Astrid to her presence. Astrid's eyes welled up with tears. Gabriel's gaze flicked from Astrid to Nyx. *Why is she looking at her that way?*

Then it dawned on him. This was why she was here. It wasn't for Ein, it was for Nyx. Although he hadn't seen it before, there was a slight resemblance. The subtle shape of their noses was the same and they had similar eyes. It was so minute that it was almost unnoticeable, but he could see it now that they were both in the same room. Nyx was Astrid's daughter.

Meanwhile, Astrid's demeanor had completely changed. She no longer looked like a woman on the warpath. Her eyes were wide and tears rolled down her cheeks, but she didn't wipe her eyes. She just stared at Nyx. Meanwhile, Gabriel was just standing there, completely dumbfounded. He was so shocked by this revelation, he didn't even do anything.

As Astrid was standing there, leaving herself wide open, another fighter flew into the room. Jin kicked off the far wall and landed a devastating spinning kick to the back of Astrid's head, dropping her to the ground. Astrid's head hit the floor so hard that she actually bounced off it and slid forward. Jin landed and looked back at Gabriel and then at Nyx.

"We should move," Jin said.

"No, wait!" Gabriel held out a hand.

"What do you mean 'wait?'" Jin raised an eyebrow.

Astrid had started to stir. She put one hand on the ground and slowly pushed herself up. Gabriel was surprised that she was even able to move after that blistering strike.

She must have caught herself or something with her shadows, he thought. "I have an idea. Follow me."

Jin and Nyx followed Gabriel down the hall, away from the fight. When they got to the corner, Gabriel turned around and saw Astrid was up and following them now.

Good, she's following us.

He turned and kept going. They ran to the next turn in the hallway and looked back again. Still she was following them. Gabriel knew where they were going, but Kaze and Nyx were completely unsure of what Sentry was planning. Down the next hall, they ran into Jake, who was no longer fighting. He looked back at them, confused.

"Where are yo—"

Gabriel cut him off. "No time. Just follow me."

After coming to another turn, they looked back. Astrid was running after them now. Now that she was moving more aggressively, it was time to get out of dodge. Gabriel pointed to a wall that was covered in tinted windows. He turned to Nyx. "Teleport us right outside those windows."

She gave him a confused look.

"Just do it," he said. "Trust me."

"All right."

They were outside the building now, unable to see Astrid, but Gabriel knew that she was right on the other side. He turned and started to run.

A second later, the glass behind them shattered. Astrid jumped through it, her shadow energy breaking the way for her. She charged at them in a dead sprint.

"Why aren't we fighting her?" he asked, risking a glance over his shoulder.

"Just follow the plan," Gabriel said. "Nyx, teleport us again. A little further into the field. Across the road over there if you can. Keep us close enough for her to see, but too far for her to get to us."

Nyx nodded, somewhat understanding what he was up to now. She summoned a shadow portal, and they jumped through.

They appeared on the far side of the road near a field. In the distance, they could see Astrid, probably a football field's length away. Close enough to see them, but she couldn't attack from this range.

Gabriel nodded to them. "We keep moving."

Now, onto the next phase of his plan.

FILE #23

THE LURE

Astrid had chased after them into the woods, but now realized she didn't even know where she was. Even worse, her targets were gone.

"Team, call off the attack," she said. "We have a new objective."

"But.." Yui started to say, but she caught herself. Astrid didn't take second guessing her very well. "Um, should I recall the whole team back to our base?"

"It doesn't matter," she said. "I just need you, Reese, and Morgan. The rest can be on standby until we find them."

Immediately, the team was teleported out of the base. As quickly as they had struck, they vanished.

***

Meanwhile, Gabriel, Nyx, Jin, and Jake found themselves at the gas station in the next town. They grabbed water bottles and were gone in a flash.

"What was that all about?"

"Not yet," Gabriel said. "We need to get somewhere safe first."

Jin looked over across the street to see a fairly simple motel. She made a motion to it with her head, and they all agreed. So, in no time, they were checked into two adjoining rooms. They met up in one of the rooms. Nyx sat on the bed while Gabriel stood in the center of the room. Kaze stood by the window, keeping an eye on the parking lot just in case.

Jake was raiding the mini-fridge for snacks. "So?"

Gabriel looked over to Nyx. "Do you know how Astrid knows about us?"

She looked up and raised an eyebrow. "No, of course not. Why?"

"Did you see the way she looked at you?"

"I mean, yeah."

"And the resemblance?"

Nyx narrowed her eyes. "Resemblance?"

"Yeah," Gabriel said. "It was feint. But I noticed something in those few moments when she was staring at you. She looks like you, but only slightly."

Nyx lowered her head, trying to process everything. Was it possible that that woman was…No, there was no way. "When I was young, I was put up for adoption. I never knew my parents," she finally said after a few moments.

No one said anything. What could they say? What does someone say when a friend's crazy mother comes back, almost kills them, and tries to steal her daughter back? This wasn't exactly something anyone had trained them for at the Academy.

Jin looked over at Nyx, intrigued. Jake had dropped the peanuts he was eating, surprised and unsure of what to say.

Finally, Gabriel said, "When I found her in the Guild base, she had a chance to take out Ein, but she never even went for it. I think we were wrong when we assumed she was after him. I think all of this was to get to you. I think she orchestrated the attack on the Protectorate. Getting us to come after her in

Venezuela, and the attack on the base...all of it was just to get to you."

Nyx looked down. She didn't want to admit it. But she knew it was true. Something in her gut, in her soul, knew that it was true.

Ever the straightforward one, Jin asked, "So, what's the next step of the plan?"

Gabriel started pacing again. He wasn't the planning type. He was one who took action. He wasn't the one to come up with the big plan or solve mysteries. That was for people like Serena and Simon. How were they going to get out of this?

Nyx stood up and looked at Gabriel. "We can't go back to the Guild. She's been playing us this whole time. We need to do something she won't expect."

"You're right. She knows how we work because she knows the Protectorate and Ein. So, we need do think outside the box here," Gabriel said.

Jin walked over. "We need to isolate her. Get her to come to us. If we follow Guild and Protectorate protocol, she'll probably be able to track us, so we need somewhere we can lure her to, and then we can spring a trap."

Jake was chewing on some peanuts from the bar. "What about my dad's lake house?"

Everyone looked at him. His mouth was still full. "What?"

Gabriel was nodding. "That's actually not a bad idea. We go there, set a trap, and then get them to come there where we spring it on her."

Nyx held up a hand. "But how do we get her to follow us there?"

"Good point."

"Codex," Jin said. "We get Codex to leave some breadcrumbs for us. If she's tracking us online, Codex could leave some clues for her online to lead her to us. But we have to make it look legitimate. Like using a credit card at a nearby gas station or a security camera at a bank or ATM."

"Sounds good," Gabriel said. "I think it's coming together. Now Jake, are you sure we can use your dad's lake house?"

"Sure thing. He never uses it. It's something he only goes to if there is a client he wants to impress, but these days, he's usually staying at five-star hotels and other places for work. He's rarely home these days."

***

The smell of incense was heavy in the air as Astrid burned candles in her room. She was kneeling on the ground, facing a small prism and praying to the universe like she had so many times before. Few people knew she was a religious person, but she was a devote member of the Prismatic Church. The church's dogma focused on the energy of the universe and taught that energy is inside all living beings. It stressed the importance of that connection. Although it condoned violence and killing, Astrid saw it as sending those who crossed her back to the universe to return one day as another form of energy. So, to her, killing was not an evil thing.

She prayed that the universe would grant her this one request. To find her daughter and bring her back in peace.

"I never should have given her up," she whispered. "I was so young, and the world was a scary place. I never wanted to, but I thought it was better for her in the end."

She paused and just listened for a moment. Her hope was to receive some kind of answer from the universe.

"I know it was my fault. I know I should have found her once I became an adult, but a Protectorate agent isn't the best for a child. I was gone for days, no weeks, on end. Sometimes I was put in the hospital after a mission. And with no other family around, who would take care of her? No. Putting her up for adoption was the right thing."

Still no answer came.

"Please. Give me some kind of sign. Let me know I am doing the right thing. Tell me that it would be better for her to be with me than the Protectorate. With the Guild."

Just then, one of her candles winked out as the wick burned up. She looked over to it, noticed the change in light around her, then looked back at the prism and smiled. She took that as a sign that it was alright to snuff out the lights on anyone who got in her way. She interpreted that to mean she should proceed with her plan. Her path was justified.

***

The group was on their way to the cabin, opting to drive there to rest up. It was a very secluded and remote cabin in the mountains, so, they had some time to kill. Gabriel took the opportunity to call Codex.

"Hey, Simon, are you all right, man?" Gabriel asked.

"Yeah," he said. "We made it out alright. No casualties thankfully. I guess they weren't actually trying to hurt anyone specifically, just cause some distraction."

"That's good to hear. We were pretty worried."

"We?" Codex asked. "Who's we? And where are you anyway?"

"That's the thing man. We, meaning Kaze, Nyx, and Brimstone have a situation on our hands."

"What do you mean?"

"I know what Astrid is up to. She isn't after Ein. She's after Nyx. Nyx is her daughter."

There was a pause and Gabriel heard the phone hit the ground. Simon fumbled to pick it back up. "N-no way. That means this whole thing was a long con?"

"Yeah, once we realized it, we put that together. She's been playing with us the whole time."

"So…" Codex was quiet. "What do you need from me?"

"This isn't exactly an official mission, so we need you to keep this low key. Can you do that for me?"

Codex gulped. He didn't like the idea of breaking the rules. He was a rule-follower through and through. But after a moment's contemplation, he finally said, "Okay. For you guys, I will."

"We need you to leave a trail for us. Something that the Guild and Protectorate won't track or find, but Astrid will be able to."

"You mean a digital one?" he asked.

"Exactly," said Gabriel.

"Wait, you want her to find you guys?"

"Yes. We're going to set a trap for her."

"I hope you know what you are doing, Sentry. This sounds dangerous."

"It will be." Gabriel gulped. "It most certainly will be."

He could hear Codex typing feverishly on his computer. The sound of the mouse clicking as Codex worked his magic gave Gabriel hope.

"All right," Codex said after a moment of rapid computer work. "I'm going to leave a few, very subtle clues online for her to find you, but I'll make sure that the Protectorate doesn't locate you."

"Fantastic," said Gabriel. "And Codex...."

"Yes?"

"Thank you. I know this isn't easy for you, breaking the rules and all. But I think this is the way we catch her and stop this. Thank you for trusting us."

"You're welcome." He paused for a moment. "Now, go get ready, I have some work to do. Let me know when you want her to arrive."

"You got it."

Codex got to work, planting false clues to keep Astrid and her team busy while Gabriel and the others got themselves ready. Codex left little traces of them online. First, he left a fake credit card tied to Jake purchasing a rental car. Next, he showed her Gabriel making transaction at a gas station in a nearby town. Then he implanted a false security camera picture of Jin at a bank.

He looked around the room to make sure no one was watching him. No one could trace him or see what he was doing. His computer was literally untouchable. So, he knew there would be no evidence of what he was doing online. However, if someone actually did see him, that would be a different story. He would just need to make sure he wasn't caught in the act.

FILE #24

THE CABIN

When they pulled up to the cabin, everyone was impressed. It wasn't just a beautiful landscape. The cabin itself was just shy of being a mansion. Although Gabriel knew Jake's father was wealthy, he didn't realize he was this level of rich. The property had a massive circular driveway with a fountain at the center of it along with a four-car garage. The front consisted of a large stonework patio and two huge doors with glass paneling around it.

As they entered, they realized it was bigger than they'd thought with high ceilings and a big open-floor plan. Large windows covered the walls, giving them a view of the forest and the nearby lake. The decor was rustic but refined.

"Wow," said Nyx. "It looks like your dad had an expensive decorator furnish this place, huh?"

"Yeah, he usually spares no expensive with these places."

Gabriel put down his bag and looked around. Just then, an old woman came into the foyer from the kitchen. She had a weathered face and thick, curly hair in a bun. She wore a flannel shirt and rough jeans. Her large boots were covered in dirt from years of work outside.

"Well, I'll be," she said. "Jake Burns, didn't know you were coming for a visit."

"Pickles? I didn't know you were still working out here!" Jake rushed over to give the groundskeeper a big hug.

She returned the embrace with two hardy pats on the back. She let him go and held him so she could give him a look. "Let's me take a look at you. My how you've grown, kiddo."

"I'm not a kid anymore, Pickles. I'm an adult."

"No, can't be. You're what sixteen...seventeen?"

He chuckled. "No, I'm twenty-three now."

"Get outta town! How'd that happen?"

"That's just how it works, Pickles."

She grabbed him for another embrace. "Well, who are your friends."

Jake gestured to all of them. "Well, uh, Pickles, these are my coworkers and friends, and we're in trouble, actually. You know my job, right?"

"Yes, your father told me. You work for the Protectorate, right?"

"Yeah, and we have someone after us. So, we need a safe place to hide so it might be safer for you to leave."

"Not burning likely," she said firmly. "This is as much my home as it is yours. And you, you're like a son to me. If you're in trouble, I am stay to help. Now, tell me what you need me to do."

So, they gave her a simplified version of the story. Despite the situation, Pickles wasn't swayed at all. She was determined to stay and help. She was the kind of woman that looked at every problem as if it was just a challenge; someone who saw a mountain in front of them as just the next step in her day. Jake had forgotten how tenacious she was. It had been a long time since he'd seen her, let alone been to the cabin.

Jake finally remembered to introduce the group to Pickles. "Oh, Pickles, this is Jin, Gabriel, and Cadence."

An hour later, after taking some time to rest, the group met back up to plan their next move. The first thing they did was walk the grounds and Pickles showed them around. She took them up the mountain, around the lake, and even to the caves nearby. While they walked Nyx asked, "Jake, is her name really Pickles?"

"No, I mean, not really. When I was little, my mom, dad, and I spent a lot of time at the cabin. Pickles was our groundskeeper and my favorite person. But I couldn't say her name as a little kid. So, I guess I called her Pickles. Now, twenty years later, the name stuck."

"Oh, that's adorable," she whispered, grinning.

"Yeah, she actually loved it. She has everyone call her Pickles now. Even people she's just met."

Nyx contained a squeal. She saw her friend in a new light. Normally, Jake was all big talk and bravado. She'd never seen this side of him before. She smiled shyly. When he turned to look back at her, she averted her eyes. She tried to make it look like she was looking out at the surrounding cave formations.

As they started to make their way back to the house, Pickles turned to the crew. "Well, I think that's about it. So, what's the plan?"

"Since shadow is her main source of power, we need to try and nullify her tactical advantage," said Gabriel.

"So, we need light?" Jin asked.

Gabriel snapped his fingers. "Exactly."

"We have some flares and fireworks, actually."

"Fireworks?" asked Jake.

"Well, the town does a big firework display over the lake for the Fourth of July. It's a big to-do, if you know what I mean. So, they store them here and fire them down by the water on our property."

"Flares and fireworks. All right, that could work," said Gabriel.

"We also have some propane tanks for the cook out this summer," Pickles added.

"What about cars?" asked Jake. "Does my dad still keep several cars in the garage."

Pickles pressed a button on her phone and the garage doors all started to open. Inside were eight cars, two in each of the four garages. There were some off-road vehicles, an all-terrain vehicle, two trucks, a sports car, and a couple sports utility vehicles. She smiled. "Yeah, there are a few cars here. Not sure what you have planned, but there they are."

Gabriel gave Jake a sly grin. "Those could come in handy."

Jin looked over at the cars. Behind the four wheelers, she could see a large set of outdoor lights. They were the high-powered kind that could light up a football field. Each one had eight large bulbs attached to a mechanical platform on top of large wheels.

"Are those for the firework display as well?" she asked, pointing to the lights.

"Oh, no, actually," said Pickles. "Those are for outdoor parties Mr. Burns throws on occasion. They are so powerful, he usually sets them up over by the tree line, and they light up the whole area."

"Think we could use 'em?" asked Jake, impressed.

"I don't see why not," she replied.

"I think we have enough resources here to make this work. Should we get started?"

Everyone agreed, and they got underway.

Jin and Gabriel decided to work on the inside with Pickles while Jake and Nyx worked on the outside traps.

While near the forest, Nyx looked at Jake. "Thank you."

"For what?"

She shifted awkwardly. "For helping me with this crazy situation."

He looked at her, a little befuddled. "Why wouldn't we help you?"

"I don't know. This isn't really your fight."

"Yes, it is. This woman is going after one of my friends and teammates. So, it's as much my fight as anyone else's."

She got a little teary at hearing that. Normally, she wasn't an emotional person. Years in the foster system and then living with adoptive parents had taught her to keep her thoughts and emotions in check. Her adoptive parents were great, but there was something about being adopted—about being picked by someone and hoping that they would take you away from the orphanages—that made someone a little more guarded.

But this whole situation had her all mixed up and confused. There was a part of her that hated her mother. There was a part of her that was confused about why she was doing this. Didn't Astrid care about her? The other part of her wanted to call this whole thing off and run away with Astrid to forget this life and maybe find happiness. But then again, maybe that happiness was right in front of her.

"We all have our own battles, you know, Cadence?" Jake paused and let out a long sigh. "Like, I've been dealing with my own demons for a while now. I finally decided I needed help and started going to therapy. It's honestly been a lot of help for me."

"Oh, I…uh…I didn't know."

He smirked. "It's not a big deal. It isn't this taboo thing. We all have some stuff going on in our heads, and therapy has been really good for me. I mean, who couldn't use someone to talk to?"

"That's a good point. Maybe I should see someone after all of this is done."

Jake nodded. "I mean, you'll most definitely have to see a Protectorate-appointed counselor, but you should see someone more long-term if you need to. You can see my therapist, if you want. I'll give you his number if you want."

"That sounds like a good idea," Nyx said.

She smiled at him for a long while. He was busy tying a knot so he didn't notice. Jake definitely wasn't the meathead she thought he was when she'd met him during the Zero incident. He had a lot more depth than she'd realized. He seemed like he had a good heart too.

Inside, Jin came downstairs to find Gabriel. She leaned down and looked at him. Her eyes were intense, and it caught him off guard. "Are you all right?" he asked.

She stood up and looked around. "This is going to be dangerous, you know?"

"Yeah, well that kind of comes with the job. You aren't afraid, are you?" In all his time knowing Jin, he had never once seen her look afraid. She was the most stoic, confident person he knew.

"No, it's more of a mental thing. I wonder if this is the best plan."

"Well, it might not be the best plan, but I think if we go through our normal channels, Astrid is likely to catch us. By staying off the grid, we have a chance to trick her for a change."

Jin sighed. "That's true. I just can't help but wonder about all of this here."

"I think the traps will give us an edge, plus we have you and Jake on our team. So, I think we're in good hands."

Jin didn't catch on that Gabriel had just complimented her. "Jake and I aren't some super power that can swing the tide of battle like you may think. The people we are going up against are very powerful. Especially, Astrid. She is S-tier, for sure."

"Then I'll fight her myself if I have to," he said, staring into her eyes.

Her returning glare was like ice. A shiver went down his back. She had that cold, calculating expression that he had come to know. She was quite the powerful presence.

"What will you do if it's just you and her?" Jin finally asked after a moment of staring him down.

"I will fight to my last breath. I don't care what happens to me, but I'm not about to let this person hurt my friends. My family."

Jin narrowed her eyes at him, unsure if he was being sincere or not. But knowing Gabriel, she thought he probably was. He was the naivest person she had ever met. He still clung to that notion that he could change the world. Something she knew was impossible. The world was a messed up, broken place, and she knew that.

But still, Gabriel Green was convinced that he alone could save them all. Maybe it wasn't naivety. Maybe he was just a fool.

"Fine," she said. "We will see what happens, Gabriel Green."

After all the traps were laid and the plan was prepared, the team reconvened in the main living room and went over their plans one last time. While everyone left to get ready, Sentry contacted Codex.

"Remember, once I leave the final breadcrumb, they'll be there almost instantly. They have a teleporter, so it'll be pretty much right away. Are you guys sure you are ready?"

Gabriel let out a big sigh, preparing himself. "Yes, we are all set to go."

"Here goes nothing," Codex answered. "Best of luck."

FILE #25

ASSAULT

Astrid returned from her prayer alter to check up on Reese. As their resident computer expert, he was in charge of tracking them. Reese was in front of a massive computer screen made up of multiple smaller ones. Each individual monitor was running a different system or program to locate them. He was running through all manner of online sources, looking for clues. A few actually had some information, but the majority were pulling up nothing.

"Any leads?" Astrid asked as she pulled a chair up beside him.

"A few. We have a receipt from a card that Jake Burns has on file. So, it looks like they rented a car here," he said, pointing to the map.

"Do we know where they were headed?"

"Yes, actually," he said. "We have a hit from a security camera with the license plate here."

"Any known hideouts there for the Guild?"

"No," he said. "Based on the information that Morgan stole when she was inside the Guild base, we don't believe there is one in that area. We don't know if they're stopping yet. But I just got another hit at a gas station. They got gas in this small remote town near the mountains."

"Show me," she said.

Reese showed her the receipt of the online transaction.

"Any hits on locations there?"

"Well, what's odd is that they didn't get a lot of gas there. See the price?" he asked.

"So, they aren't going far," she said. "Run a search for any known hideouts tied to those four agents."

"I just started it."

A moment later, there was a hit. A picture popped up on one of the monitors of a beautiful cabin in the woods. It was the picture of a well-known man, an internet celebrity that apparently was related to Jake. Astrid stood up. "So, they're going there."

"Mostly likely. We should move quickly—"

Astrid was already on her way out the door. He turned around and grabbed his laptop, chasing after her. As she rounded the corner, she saw Yui and Morgan. "Get the team together. We have a lead."

"We do?" asked Morgan.

"Where to?" asked Yui.

"Once we get the team together, we will be going in hot," she said. "Yui, do as much research as you can on this address."

Yui took the paper from Astrid and instantly started researching a place to teleport them. Morgan turned and fell in step with Astrid. "Are you sure that's how you want to handle this?" she asked.

Astrid had fear in her eyes, something that Morgan hadn't seen before. She looked like she would break down at a moment's notice. "I am not losing my daughter again. Either we do this right, or we don't get another shot of it. If this fails, I don't know what I'll do."

Morgan had never seen her like this before. Astrid was always cool-headed and calculating. She was even a little standoffish. This was a new side of her. She actually looked emotional for a change. As they walked down the corridor, she even saw Astrid's hand was shaking a little. Morgan tried to focus herself. If her boss was this uptight about the situation, she would need everyone on their game.

Within no time, the team was assembled. Yui stood in the office that looked down over the group. She liked to have an aerial view of the team she was about to send so she could see everyone at once. She couldn't quite explain it, but sight was important to her gift. After surveying the team, she pressed the button on the intercom and said, "Ready team?"

Astrid nodded her head. "Let's do this, Yui."

So, Yui prepared herself and then summoned all her strength for this next teleportation. She would send them in two groups. She could send large teams, but not all of them at once. As such, Astrid and her team appeared in the forest at the end of a long, winding gravel path that led to the house. The other team popped into the forest on the other side of the house. The teams would move through the woods and approach the house from both sides to surround them.

"Move out!" Astrid and Morgan said in unison. The teams fanned out to cover more ground. The few tanks they did have spearheaded each group. The blasters, those with projectile abilities, moved in behind them.

The tree line was so thick that they couldn't actually see the house and the darkness made it difficult to move through the woods, but, they could tell they were going in the right direction because Morgan and Astrid had GPS tracking devices on their wrists. They both moved in the direction of the house at a slow pace.

Just then, Morgan heard what sounded like a tree snapping in half, and one of her men was smacked in the chest by a heavy log. He was sent flying backwards and knocked unconscious. She looked surprised.

Her team looked at her, but she just pointed forward, so, they continued on. Suddenly, another snap could be heard. Like before, a log smashed into one of her team, sending someone through the air.

"Astrid, we have traps on our side," Morgan said.

"Copy. We have them here as well."

"Do we proceed?"

"Of course, we do!"

Morgan winced from the yell coming through her ear piece. She looked at her team and motioned them forward. They were not backing down now. Not because of a few simple traps.

"Move carefully, team."

Each team moved through the woods, narrowly avoiding the traps when they could. A few of their members still got knocked out by swinging branches or other traps. One fell into a ditch, two were caught in rope traps, and a few had their feet cut up by spike traps and were unable to carry on.

Finally, the teams came to the edge of the forest and were finally able to see the cabin. Their numbers were smaller, but they were nothing to sneeze at.

Explosions and crackling bangs came from all around them. Some of the team members preemptively fired off their attacks. A blast of purple energy shot through the forest, causing a tree to fall. Several of their team retreated and several were caught in another blast. A few hit each other in the confusion. Firecrackers continued to explode around them, causing some of them to panic further. As they started to dwindle, the teams realized what had happened.

They were once again the butt of the joke. Another trap had sprung, and they had been caught in the fire.

Astrid called over to Morgan through their headsets. "We lost about seven on our side. You?"

"Nine, ma'am. A few too many, if you ask me."

"Some of them must have forgotten their training," Astrid said, pointedly looking at some of her team. They looked away in embarrassment.

"Indeed," said Morgan.

"Team," Astrid said. "Move in."

The team readied themselves. As they moved, they noticed several of the cars parked out on the lawn. At first, Astrid was suspicious that this might be another trap. She motioned for two of the members to check them out, but the cars weren't actually rigged to explode or anything.

While several of Astrid's team was inspecting the cars, Jin made her move. Nyx teleported her behind the enemies so she could sneak up behind them. She made a point to avoid Astrid, who would be able to sense her if she got too close, and moved in on Morgan's side. She attacked the ones from the rear first, knocking out two of the troops and carefully laying them down before moving through the rest.

Finally, after downing quite a few enemies, one was able to avoid her attack. They must have sensed her with their gift, but she moved in to try and finish her off.

"We got a bogie!" yelled the woman.

Jin grimaced as she swept the woman's legs out from under her and delivered an elbow to her back. She'd knocked her out, but the damage was done. She had been exposed and could hear footsteps all around her. The enemies were converging on her. Jin slunk down and hid under one of the cars, whispering into her earpiece. "I'm blown. Get me out of here, Nyx."

She needed to move. The enemies were closing in, and she didn't want to be there when they arrived. So, she moved. Crawling around to the other side of the car, she hoped to avoid her attackers.

A few rushed past her without seeing her. She then crawled under another car. Just as she was about to call out to Nyx again, she saw her exit. Before her, a portal appeared in the shadow of one of the cars, but there was a problem. A group of guards stood between her and the portal. She could attack them and expose herself or she could sneak around them. Whatever she did, she would need to move quickly. Then an idea came to her.

She slid out from under the car and moved quietly toward them. When she was almost to them, she jumped up and knocked out the first guard before they heard her. The other two saw her out of the corner of their eyes. She delivered a throat punch to the first and dodged the sonic blast from the second. Jumping behind the guard who was holding his throat, she pushed him forward, using him like a human shield. The other guard shot out another sonic blast, but it hit the human shield. She knocked them both to the ground and then delivered a karate chop to the back of their necks.

Now, there was nothing between her and the portal.

"She's over there!" came a voice from behind.

Jin, moving as fast as her codename suggested, bolted to the shadow portal, sliding to it as the enemy swarmed around her.

Then she was gone.

Morgan's team had missed her by mere seconds. But Kaze had done her job, their team was down to just a few more troops.

As Jin appeared beside her team, Nyx gave her a thumbs up.

"Nice work," said Gabriel.

"My turn," Jake said.

FILE #26

THE SHADOW STRIKES

Astrid had heard the ruckus from Morgan's side, but the cabin stood between them so she couldn't see them. She called to Morgan in her earpiece, but she didn't respond right away.

Finally, Morgan responded. "We were hit, Astrid. We got ambushed by two or three of them."

"Are you sure?" Astrid asked.

"I don't know. No one got a good look at them, but it had to have been a team. They moved really quickly."

Maybe it was someone like Trei. He alone could have done that. Recalling the intel they'd stolen, there was another member of the Guild with the same ability. A new agent codenamed Kaze.

Could she have done this alone? she wondered. Unlikely, but possible. Astrid didn't want to assume anything, but it didn't matter in the end. They would stick to the plan.

Jake pressed a button, turning on every car's headlight and sounding every car's alarm. Astrid's team was instantly thrown into a panic. Some moved away from the cars, expecting them to explode. But instead of setting explosives, Jake launched a fireball at the center car. The beautiful sports car erupted into a tower of fire, sending pieces flying into the air.

The invaders scrambled away. A few were hit by the shrapnel. One was even run over by the large wheels that shot off of it.

Then the next car exploded. In quick succession, Jake caused all the cars to explode.

Boom! Boom! Boom!

Each one sent sparks and metal into the air. Astrid protected herself, but most of her team was caught up in the explosions. While she'd remained unscathed, the intense explosions had affected her shields. Her shadows had been weakened, but it wasn't enough to worry about.

Both teams met in front of the cabin. They were down to a handful of their troops. Astrid was fuming now. Morgan was worried about what she might do. When Astrid became angry, there was only one outcome and Morgan didn't want to be on the receiving end of it.

Astrid looked at her troops. "Focus fire on the cabin. Make an entrance."

Inside, Gabriel and his team took cover as energy, fire, and other projectiles slammed into the wall. The building lurched as blasts of energy tore through the side. Beams of plasma shattered pillars and scorching rays melted metal.

"Everyone watch out!" Gabriel screamed. He threw a shield up, trying to keep them together. After a few minutes, the assault slowed down until it came to an end. He waited a moment before dropping his shield.

Jin peered through a small hole in the wall. "Looks like we have about six of them left. Astrid is at the rear."

"What's next?" Jake asked.

"We move to the next phase of the plan," Gabriel said, looking over at Nyx for confirmation.

She thought for a second and then exhaled, forcing the thought from her mind, and nodded. It had to be done. It was the only way to end this all. She wanted to bring this nightmare to a close and never think of it again.

"Let's do it," Nyx said.

Gabriel took a deep breath. This would be hard. They didn't have their ace in the hole, Serena. Serena's mental link would've allowed them to work in unison perfectly. This would be a much less coordinated attack, but hopefully, their plan would work.

Nyx got ready to summon her portal just as Jake stood up and fired a large flame blast into the center of the enemies. They all scattered. That was Nyx's signal.

She summoned the portal and Gabriel and Kaze jumped through, appearing behind their enemies. Kaze struck first while Gabriel took a defensive stand. Before any of the troops could guard themselves, Jin, moving like the wind, delivered a devastating elbow to one of the guards's faces. The other got a knee to the gut. One actually got an attack off, but Gabriel slammed him with a TK burst and he went flying into a nearby tree.

Morgan attacked Jin with a jump kick. Jin just narrowly avoided in. Morgan swung high and low, trying to hit Jin, but she couldn't land a single one. Shifting to use her gift, she glared at Jin.

"Do you know why they called me Agent Raven?" she asked.

"No," Jin said.

"In my culture, Raven was a trickster god. It could shapeshifter and become anyone. That's what I did to you friend. Agent Hardlight, I believe his name was."

"So, that's how Astrid got into the Guild! You pretended to be him, and you got her inside?" Jin gasped.

"Indeed. Not only does my gift allow me to shift parts of my body"—Morgan tranformed her hands into blades—"but I can also shapeshift into people now. I've had my gifts elevated."

"What does that even mean?" Jin asked.

"I guess I can tell you since you'll be dead in a few minutes. I had my gifts enhanced by the Limit Breaker."

Jin didn't know who or what that was, but she didn't like the sound of that. Someone or something that could enhance gifts could be dangerous. But before she could ask a follow-up question, the former agent lunged at her with her blade hands and swung a glancing blow that could have taken her head off.

Meanwhile, Gabriel was defending against the other heavy hitter. Astrid. She lunged at him with her shadow blades. Large, swirling tendrils of shadow shaped like swords lashed out at him in an almost endless barrage.

He didn't think he could keep this up. Just like their fight in the Guild base, all he could do was defend. But fortunately, that was when the next step of the plan kicked in. As she attacked, Nyx teleported Jake to the large outdoor lights that Jin had found in the garage. After uncovering all three of them, Jake activated them one at a time. Thanks to her teleportation, Nyx was able to get him to each one quickly.

The light was blinding after the initial darkness and, for a moment, no one could see. But Sentry was ready for it. In the split second, while his eyes adjusted, he pushed out with a surge of telekinetic energy, using it to sense the surrounding area. Once he could tell where Astrid was, he made his move. He pushed forward, trying to knock her down, but Astrid absorbed the blow and rolled backward. In a flash, she was back on her feet.

Still momentarily blinded, she shot out with her shadows. But nothing happened. Her shadows had been nullified by the intense lights.

Her eyes began to adjust and she realized the situation once she saw the lights. "Well played," she said to no one in particular.

Gabriel smiled when he heard that. He knew they had her. Pushing forward, he had her moving on the defensive now.

Since the intense lights made summoning a shadow portal impossible, Gabriel had to hold his own for some time until Jake could back him up. This was the one flaw in their plan.

At first, Gabriel appeared to have the edge, but while he was attacking, she was enacting her own plan. Dodging his attacks, she was eventually close enough to summon a shadow behind the first light and slash at it. The bulb fell to the ground, creating a small shadowed area. The rest of the open field was still bathed in light so she still needed to remove the rest of the lights.

In a fury, Gabriel attacked. He couldn't believe that she'd gotten an attack off from that distance. He was mentally kicking himself now for allowing that to happen.

How does she have that much control?

If only he was stronger, he might've been able to stop her. If this whole thing failed, it was on him.

With his body surrounded in telekinetic energy, he punched and kicked at her, allowing himself to get little too close. She could tell he was angered. Of course he was. He was playing right into her hands.

Then, in one fell swoop, she attacked. But his body was too well shielded. Combined with the light, her shadows were still too weak.

Gabriel slammed her with a wall of TK energy, sending her rolling backwards. He thought he had her. Suddenly, he heard another light crash to the ground. She was halfway to completely shrouding the field in darkness once again, and then she would be unstoppable.

Her attacks doubled in strength and she unleashed a flurry of attacks. It was like being attacked by a million daggers. Gabriel was barely able to stay on his feet. One shadow broke through, slicing through his side. He dropped to the ground, holding his side and putting pressure on the wound. The shadow blades were all like pointed tentacles, swinging and slashing from every direction. Another got through, slicing his leg open.

He used his hand to apply pressure on his leg, but the pain was pulling at his attention, making it hard to keep focus on his TK shield. If he didn't refocus, he was done for.

Astrid was watching in delight. Her technique with this one was working. She referred to this method as ten-thousand cuts. Instead of trying to use blunt force, she would send out thousands of little strikes, waiting for one to get through.

This young man seemed to be quite strong, but his weakness was that he lacked finesse. He couldn't keep every angle guarded at once. Just then another strike landed. A few seconds later, another got through. Then another. Soon he would bleed out.

Gabriel dropped to the ground, holding his wounds. It was all he could do to keep them all from bleeding. While on his knees, he looked up at Astrid. She was partially hidden by shadow after having taken out enough of the lights.

I failed, he thought to himself. *Or maybe not...*

"It seems you aren't up to snuff, Sentry," Astrid said.

"Well, I would say you're right. But you aren't really right. This whole plan was just to keep you busy for him." He nodded in Jake's direction.

Just as he did so, Jake landed beside her and delivered a strong punch to her jaw. He was seething with rage. The whole time he'd been running, he had to helplessly watch her slash away at his friend. Fortunately, Gabriel had been strong enough to withstand the assault.

Although Jake had learned to keep his rage in check, he knew that sometimes he needed to unleash that fury on his enemies. This was one of those times.

"Now you fight me!" he screamed as she dropped to one knee.

FILE #27

THE FLAME

As he lay helpless on the ground, Gabriel shifted his gaze to Jin. Jin was trying to hold her own against Morgan. Nyx was the only thing making a difference in the fight. Morgan was blocking Jin's attacks with bone shields while attacking with her blade hands. It was almost useless to fight her.

However, on top of her incredible reflexes and movements, Jin was able to teleport away thanks to Nyx. It hadn't been part of the initial plan, but when Nyx saw Jin flailing in the fight, she'd decided to alter the plan a little.

Her friends were doing so much for her. They were risking themselves to protect her. She had to help them. Even though they'd told Nyx to stay hidden in the cabin, she couldn't do that so she helped Jin as best she could. Fortunately, it was enough to give Kaze just the slightest edge in their fight. Something she needed.

It hurt Jin's pride tremendously to admit it, though. Kaze was a professional. She was a warrior. As such, her pride made it hard to admit when she needed help. She had been on so many combat missions, but she'd never faced someone like this.

Morgan was so strong. The way she had complete control over her entire form. The way she was able to change the makeup of her body, and how she could change it to any form. It was too much. Offense, defensive, counter attack—you name it, she could do it.

Now, Kaze had to figure out a way to use her new advantage to win.

Meanwhile, Jake was holding his own, but it was tenuous at best. The fire surrounding his hands was a great defense against shadow. He didn't quite understand what he was doing because he was just reacting instinctually, but it was working

Astrid unleashed another swarm of attacks. This time, Jake launched a flame burst in front of himself. It exploded around him, melting the shadow strike to nothing. But while he was able to stop her attacks, he couldn't land any of his own.

"Brimstone!" Gabriel yelled. "You need to go supernova!"

"What does that even mean?" Jake yelled back.

"Your hands. See how they're covered in fire? You need that everywhere!"

It took Jake a few miuntes, but eventually it dawned on him. His fire was keeping her at bay and he needed to turn up the heat.

His normal external body temperature was hot to the touch, but he needed to make it flammable. He needed to make it so the air around himself burned on contact. He needed to reach a level that he and Gabriel had only talked about during training. Something he hadn't managed quite yet.

"Brimstone, if you don't stop this woman now. I'm going to bleed out right now and die. You need to end it!"

That was the kick that Jake needed. He screamed as his body ignited into flames. The specially designed suit that Duo had made for him vented the heat, allowing it to pass through it without burning it.

With another scream, Brimstone attacked. Astrid was unable to counter him now. All of her attacks melted in the light of his flames. Her shadows were unable to withstand the light.

This was the agent that she should have neutralized. When Morgan had infiltrated the team, this was the one that they should have worried about.

Jake delivered attack after attack and all of them were landing now. Astrid kept trying to protect herself with shadow shields, but Jake broke through each one, the light from his flames weakening and then evaporating the shadows around him.

From a distance it looked like a human flame was fighting her. He was unstoppable now. Gabriel smiled as he fell to the ground. "You got this, buddy…"

Astrid fell to the ground as Jake landed another punch. She crawled backward. "Please…All I wanted was my daughter."

"You think kidnapping her was the right thing to do?"

"I didn't have any other choice! She is my only living family. I had to get to her and get her out!"

"No, you didn't. She is an adult, and she can make her own decisions!"

"You're brainwashed, just like she is. You don't understand."

Jake shook his head. Astrid took the opportunity to deliver a sneak attack, and while his head was momentarily turned, she summoned two tendrils of shadow. The spear-like ends shot down at him. However, despite being distracted, Jake's flames incinerated the shadows. Each tendril evaporated like water under the intense light of his inferno.

"Nice try," he said. "But it's over. I am the direct counter to your gift."

Astrid wouldn't accept it. She refused to allow herself to go down this way. Maybe it was a lifetime of success or never being challenged in this way. Maybe it was because of Nyx and Astrid's mad desire to get to her daughter. Whatever the reason, she lashed out in a fury, unleashing all of her power. Shadows swirled around her, striking out in every direction. She pushed out with all of her might, striking at Jake, Gabriel, and Jin. She sliced through branches and knocked down whole trees. Parts of the cabin collapsed around them.

Gabriel, despite being barely conscious, saw the attacks coming for them next. Although he wasn't sure he could manage it, he needed to protect himself and his team. Realizing he had a few flairs, he slammed them into the ground between himself and the team. Each one burst into light, burning his eyes. The intense flares devoured the shadows around him.

With one last effort, he threw a couple toward Nyx and Kaze before passing out from blood loss.

Jin was dodging Astrid's attacks. Oddly enough, so was Morgan. Out of the blue, Reese appeared. He grabbed Morgan and teleported out of the area. Jin looked on, impressed but she was also a little envious. Morgan was now safe and she was stuck trying to dodge the literal darkness around her. It was almost impossible, but dodging was literally her greatest skill so she would make due. The flare didn't hurt either.

Meanwhile, Jake remained impervious to Astrid's attacks. He tried to move between her and everyone else, but he couldn't stop all her attacks. She continued to slice through parts of the cabin and the surrounding forest. He growled. "Stop!"

But she was like a thrashing animal, screaming and lashing out in anger, refusing to be restrained. He yelled in frustration. He had her all but defeated, but he couldn't keep her attacks from doing so much damage to everyone else. He had to take her down before she tore his friends apart.

In one last effort, he summoned as much power as he could. All his anger and frustration boiled inside him until he reached his bursting point. Then he rushed at her, flaring out his flames and suppressing her shadows.

Slowly, that started to work. He grabbed her by the collar and did it again. "Enough!" he screamed, surging with burning power once again.

Just then, Nyx appeared from the shadows. Astrid looked up at her, her eyes wide like she was begging for mercy.

"Why would you do all this?" Nyx asked.

Astrid's shadows diminished and returned to her. All the damage around her ceased. It looked like a tornado had ripped through the area. The cabin was barely standing. Only the back corner was unharmed. The surrounding trees were felled and cut up into pieces. Large swaths of ground had big slices cut through it. Pickles would have a heart attack when she saw the damage.

Astrid dropped to her knees, looking at Nyx. "Because I wanted to free you from this life. The Protectorate is corrupt. It's a broken system that needs to be torn down so we can start over."

"If you wanted to have a relationship with me, you should have talked to me. Not killed, schemed, and tried to kidnap me! This was all too much."

"But the Protectorate brainwashed you. They made you—"

"I'm not brainwashed. I believe in the work I'm doing. I know the Protectorate isn't perfect. No human organization is. But I want to make it better. I want to leave this world better than I found it."

Astrid slumped to the ground and hung her head. "You will never understand. People like Ein are using you. They have tricked you into using your gifts for them."

Nyx shook her head. "I think it's you who doesn't understand. Some of us still believe in people. In the gifted. We believe we can help the world. But you...I feel sorry for you."

Astrid made eye contact with Nyx. They stared at each other for a long time. Nyx might have been afraid if it weren't for Jake radiating light around her and Astrid. Yes, Astrid could form shadows, but the light immediately nullified them if they got too close. With Jake so amped up, Astrid was powerless.

"It's over now," Nyx said. She almost added the word "mom," but she caught herself. She hadn't used that word in a long time, and she had never used it with her birth mother.

Astrid nodded in response, accepting her fate. Now she would have to face the punishment for her crimes.

FILE #28

THE NEXT PHASE

A few minutes later, Nyx had teleported the Guild team to the cabin—well, what was left of it. Astrid had been apprehended. Now, she was sitting in cell designed by Duo that had been equipped with high-powered lights to keep her shadow powers from working.

Gabriel and Jin remained onsite with Nyx while they were debriefed. Ein had arrived after they got their statements to figure out exactly what had happened.

"Well, give me a reason why you four disappeared to the middle of nowhere with Nyx."

"Sir, when we realized that Astrid had been one step ahead of us from the beginning, we realized we needed to think of something else. We couldn't go through normal channels anymore. She would have been ready for that." Gabriel stood up straight. "I take full responsibility for the whole thing. Any punishment should fall on me."

Ein nodded. "Oh, it will."

He gulped. "I understand."

"That being said," Ein added, "we owe you a debt of gratitude Agent Sentry. You did what many in the community thought would be impossible. You brought down the Shadow Assassin. For that, you have our thanks. But you still went against your training and the Protectorate. So, we'll discuss that later."

"I understand."

Jin stepped in. "Sir, it should be noted that Sentry—"

"We will discuss the whole situation back at base," Ein said, looking at the cabin. "So, Brimstone owns this place, huh? Shame, really. It was quite a wonderful place. I hope he had insurance."

With that, he turned and walked off. The three that were left looked at each other for a moment. They were all thinking the same thing: *How did we just survive that?*

Then Gabriel was reminded of something. He looked over at Jin. "What happened to the other one, Astrid's ally? You know, the one you were fighting before."

Jin sighed. "Well, she escaped when her ally showed up and teleported her away."

"Burn it all. So, we have more we need to go after."

She smiled at that. "It would seem so." Nyx walked over and put her arms around Gabriel and Jin.

Back at the base, everyone was brought up to speed on the whole situation. From their debriefings, it turned out that Astrid had, in fact, orchestrated the entire course of events. The attack on the Protectorate, Venezuela, and the assault on the Guild was all to get her daughter, Nyx. Ein was relieved that he wasn't the one she was after, but Nyx was less than enthused by the events of the week.

"Nyx, we recommend you see the Guild psychologist after this week. I'm sorry about what had transpired. I can't imagine what you're going through," said V.

It was clear that whatever group that Astrid was affiliated with was similar to most agencies, but they didn't have the same end goal. While agencies were trying to help the world, her agency was out for murder and profit.

"So, what do we know about this shadow agency?" asked V.

"Next to nothing," said Ein.

Codex chimed in. "Well, we know that Astrid, Reese, and Morgan were all former Protectors. They were all former agents believed to be killed in the field."

"So, this shadow group could be made up of former agents?" Ein turned to face V.

V put his hands together. "It's a very real possibility. We may have a whole new situation on our hands."

"Astrid might just be the tip of the iceberg. What does this mean?"

"We will need a minute for that," V said, tapping his nose.

Ein nodded. That was the signal that V wanted to have a private meeting to discuss that development.

"All right, everyone," said Ein a moment later. "We'll have a follow-up meeting later."

Everyone got up to leave. When Gabriel stood, Ein called him over.

"Yes, sir," he said.

"Based on all of the reports I read from Kaze, Brimstone, and Nyx, it seems you were the one who planned out Astrid's entire takedown."

"Uh, well..."

"I assume you were more articulate when you came up with the plan back at the cabin," Ein said, smiling.

"Yes sir. I just wasn't expecting that. I was honestly assuming I was about to be suspended or something."

"No, not this time, Sentry. But next time, next time might be different," Ein said. "You're a good agent. You have a good head on your shoulders and good instincts. But we need to make it look like we are handling this the right way. So, this is me reprimanding you."

"I understand, sir," he said.

Gabriel was almost to the door when Ein called out and said, "We will be having a follow-up meeting in a few minutes. We'd like you to be there with *your* team."

He was referring to the Oculus team. They hadn't had a breakthrough in some time, so maybe this new lead was related.

***

Meanwhile, Romulus was reading the reports that came through his computer screen. Mostly, the reports were mission details. As one of the committee members on the Protectorate, he was in charge of overseeing the mission parameters. Often times, he and his fellow committee members had to issue the missions. Other times, they were in charge of overseeing their completion. When a mission went poorly, they were the ones to deal with it. When there was a success, they handled that as well. The entire operation fell on the shoulders of the Protectorate committee members.

He grabbed his phone and dialed a number. "Look into the Iberian situation for me."

"We have someone looking into it," said the voice on the other end.

"No, I said I want you to look into it. Understand?"

The voice didn't answer right away. There was a decently long pause while Romulus sat there, waiting. Finally, the voice answered. "Yes, Romulus. I will be there within the hour."

"Good. And I want a report on my desk by morning. No excuses. We close this case now."

Romulus hung up the phone and leaned back. He enjoyed this position. With all the work he had done in the field, all the missions he had run, he was one of the best. Now he oversaw almost every aspect of the Protectorate. Now he was at the top. Well, almost the top. He was still under the chairman of the committee. But Dexter Romulus had his eyes set on that position next.

That was what the Oculus was for. Together, they worked to ensure that the power remained in their hands. Well, ideally, that was how it worked. There were more and more times that they backstabbed and jockeyed for position. There were those that weren't as unified as others. People like Dr. Drake, who ended up betraying them in the end. Others in the Oculus just weren't as devoted. Like Antonia Sagas, the heir to the Sagas fortune, who barely cared about the part her family left for her in the Oculus. She hadn't earned her place. She was given it. And because her parents were so wealthy, the Oculus allowed it.

Romulus sneered.

Just then, he received a call. It wasn't from his main line. It was from his cell phone. Agent Charm. He held the phone up to his ear. "Yes?"

"Sir, we captured Astrid. We are bringing her in as we speak."

"Well, that is good news. I think I should pay a visit then. Your agency certainly has been racking up the wins these days."

Charm smiled. "Thank you, sir."

"So, tell me everything."

Charm told him everything that she knew in quick order. Romulus spun a pen around his fingers while he listened. When she got to the end, he accidentally snapped it in half. He couldn't believe it. How could Astrid be captured by the most junior agents in the entire agency? It didn't make sense. She was one of the best. Maybe the best they had ever seen.

Romulus thought about what he needed to do next. How would he play this? He wondered. This situation would take a delicate hand. Would he involve the Oculus? Bartholomew Zeno? Although he had asked himself this question before, he had not come to a decision just yet. But now was the time.

He opened an email and began typing. He didn't need the Oculus. He didn't want to show weakness. If they found out about this, they would use this to get the advantage on him. He would lose influence and authority in the organization. He couldn't do that. He wouldn't allow it. He would take care of this himself.

***

Back at the Guild headquarters, the team that had signed up to find the Oculus was meeting. It had been almost a year since they embarked on this mission, but they were nowhere near close to unraveling this thread. They still had no leads, except what they had learned about the shadow agency that Astrid worked for.

"This is our only new information," said V. "This shadowy group is our next lead."

"There isn't much to go on," said Ivy.

"No, not exactly," said Serena. "But we have options."

V put a hand under his chin, a million scenarios running through his head. There were options. Despite everything, there were options. He knew it.

Ivy noticed his thoughtful expression and knew exactly what that meant. He was working out all of the angles. He would come up with a good plan. But she had her own plan for getting to the shadow agency.

"I suggest we break up into teams. Each one figure out a plan of attack."

V gave Ivy a sideways glance. He didn't know what she was planning here, but he wasn't sure he liked it. However, maybe divide and conquer was a decent plan of attack.

"All right, everyone. Let's brainstorm in teams."

So, they set out to plan a new the next phase of the operation. Everyone was hopeful now that they had a lead. V watched Ivy walk out of the room with Serena, unsure of what she was planning. For V, instinct was everything. Being able to predict an outcome was his whole gift. So, not being able to figure out what Ivy was up to made him worry.

But that was something he would have to deal with later. For now, he needed to find a way to locate the shadow agency.

Epilogue

Reese and Morgan reappeared on the top of a building. They looked around, unsure of where Yui had teleported them. They looked at each other. Reese wrapped his arms around her, hugging her tightly. Although they played the part of reluctant allies, they were actually in love. Astrid didn't know about their relationship, because if she did, they wouldn't have been permitted to work together.

He let her go and looked at her. "Are you all right?"

"Yes," she said. "I'm fine."

"What happened?"

"We lost Astrid. She let her emotions get to her."

"I've never seen anything like that before. Astrid is the coldest, most calculating person I know."

"Well, it didn't help that they planned out a perfect trap for her. We just didn't handle it right. We should have waited and planned for it. We should have taken time to figure out the best plan. But Astrid wanted us there immediately. So, we rushed in and paid the price."

Reese looked over his shoulder. He let go of her and pushed her away from him. Yui was coming through a door that led to the roof. Seeing the two of them standing there, she walked over.

"Well, Astrid is gone. I can't pull her. There's an anchor or someone keeping my teleporting from getting her."

"So, the shadow agency is now fully in his hands," Morgan said.

"Yes," said Yui. "Without Astrid, you know Quiet is already calling for a meeting. He wants you two there."

"Where is it?" Reese asked.

"Argentina," said Yui.

"Haven't been there in a while. But I guess we are getting back to his roots," said Morgan.

Morgan and Reese looked over the edge as Yui asked, "Are you ready?"

They nodded. Although they couldn't be completely certain, they were sure they were going to be in trouble. Astrid's capture and this mission as a whole wasn't something they were allowed to do. It wasn't a mission assigned by Quiet, but, it was something Astrid said she needed to do. So, they went along with it. Now, they were going to pay the price for it. Hopefully, Quiet wouldn't be too mad. But there was no telling what he would do to them.

Characters

Gabriel Green
    Codename: Sentry
    Gift: Telekinesis

Serena Hammond
    Codename: Insight
    Gift: Telepathy

Jake Burns
    Codename: Brimstone
    Gift: Fire manipulation

Simon Cruz
    Codename: Codex
    Gift: Technopathy

Cadence Veil
    Codename: Nyx
    Gift: Shadow Teleportation

Jin Kenichi
    Codename: Kaze
    Gift: Hyperkinesis

Andre Vincent
    Codename: V (formerly Victory)
    Gift: Enhanced Intuition

Darla Sweet
    Codename: Zion
    Gift: Psionic (Psychic) Weapons

Georgia Winters
   Codename: Ivy
   Gift: Botanokinesis (Plant Manipulation)

Frank Stone
   Codename: Duo
   Gift: Alchemical Bonding

Aiden McKinley
   Codename: Insomnia
   Gift: Doesn't require sleep

Hue Long
   Codename: Foundry
   Gift: Metal Manipulation

Meilin Chow
   Codename: Charm
   Gift: "Good Luck"

DeVon Santos
   Codename: DarkSky
   Gift: Weather Manipulation

Eloy Einrich
   Codename: Ein
   Gift: Time Manipulation

Antwon James
   Codename: Crimson
   Gift: Rapid Healing

Minato Kenichi
   Codename: Trei
   Gift: Hyperkinesis

Enrique Melendez
   Codename: Hardlight

Gift: Light Solidifying

Hakim Varma
    Codename: Rikers
    Gift: Air Form

Roger "Rocky" Samson
    Codename: Granite
    Gift: Terrakinesis

Barry Jenkins
    Codename: Piledriver
    Gift: Enhanced Durability

About the Author

L. D. Valencia has always loved telling stories. From playing pretend with his siblings to running Dungeons and Dragons campaigns, stories have always been his passion. It wasn't until he started his master's degree that he was convinced by a student to take his ideas to the published world.

He currently lives in the Nashville area with his lovely wife and their new son. As an educator, he hopes to inspire his students to love reading and writing. This book is a testament to that dream. Education is his goal, reading is his passion, and writing is his dream.

BOOKS BY L. D. VALENCIA

The Gifted Complex

The Burns Conflict

The Zero Crisis

The Heart Paradox

The Titan Project

Follow L. D. Valencia on Social Media:

https://www.facebook.com/ldvalenciabooks

https://www.instagram.com/l.d.valencia/

https://twitter.com/thegiftedworld

Made in the USA
Middletown, DE
20 October 2023

41126468R00120